ADVENTURES
at
WOHELO CAMP

Summer of 1928

Margaret R. O'Leary
and
Dennis S. O'Leary

iUniverse, Inc.
Bloomington

Adventures at Wohelo Camp
Summer of 1928

Copyright © 2011 Margaret R. O'Leary and Dennis S. O'Leary

Clara Hallard Fawcett created the cover artwork in 1928.

iUniverse books may be ordered through booksellers or by contacting:

iUniverse
1663 Liberty Drive
Bloomington, IN 47403
www.iuniverse.com
1-800-Authors (1-800-288-4677)

ISBN: 978-1-4620-2503-9 (sc)
ISBN: 978-1-4620-2504-6 (e)

Printed in the United States of America

iUniverse rev. date: 07/19/2011

Contents

Authors' Preface

≈⇒·◇·⇐≈

Emily Sophian O'Leary (1913–1994) passed away after a long illness at age eighty years in Kansas City, Missouri on June 13, 1994. She, like Hiiteni (pronounced high-a-Teen-ee), the founder and director of Wohelo (pronounced woe-Hee-low) camp on Lake Sebago in Maine, wished to pass on peacefully in her bed at home, but circumstances beyond her control and the control of her husband thwarted her plan. Her obituary in the *Kansas City Star* read:

> Emily Sophian O'Leary, 80, Fairway, died June 13, 1994, in Carondelet Manor [nursing home in Kansas City]. There will be no services; cremation. The family requests no flowers. Mrs. O'Leary was an assistant to the women's page editor of The Kansas City Star in the 1930s and wrote book reviews for The Star in 1970s and 1980s. She attended Smith College, the Sorbonne in Paris and the University of Missouri-Columbia. Her father was the late Dr. Abraham Sophian, a founder of Menorah Hospital. She was a lifelong area resident. Survivors include her husband of 58 years, Theodore M. O'Leary of the home, former reporter for The Kansas City Times and book reviewer for The Star; a son, Dr. Dennis S. O'Leary, St. Charles, Ill.; and six grandchildren.

Ted, Emily's husband, followed her to the grave at age ninety on February 5, 2001. His obituary read:

> Theodore M. O'Leary, 90, of Fairway, KS, passed away peacefully on February 5, 2001 following a stroke. Memorial contributions may be made to KU Endowment or to a charity of personal choice. Ted was born December 28, 1910 in Oxford, England where his parents, R.D. and Matilda O'Leary had temporarily located during his father's sabbatical. R.D. O'Leary was then Dean of the English Department at the University of Kansas. Ted grew up in Lawrence, KS, graduating from Lawrence High School and then from the University of Kansas in 1932. He was

the consummate student-athlete, junior tennis champion, record holding track star, and college basketball All American under legendary KU coach, Phog Allen. He graduated from KU as a Phi Beta Kappa and was a Rhodes Scholar candidate. Unable to find work in the journalism profession following graduation, Ted became head basketball coach at George Washington University, where he compiled an impressive record of 26 wins and 9 losses over two seasons. Deciding that coaching was not for him, he returned to Kansas City in 1934 to become a general assignment reporter for the Kansas City Times. During this time, he began to write book reviews for The Kansas City Star, a labor of love that was to continue for 60 years. In 1942, Ted became a Lieutenant Commander in the U.S. Navy, where he served stateside through the conclusion of WWII. Following the war, he became editor of "Profitable Hobbies," a magazine for aspiring inventors and entrepreneurs. Over the ensuing decade, he engaged in a progressively expanding range of freelance writing activities. These included knowledgeable summaries in the World Book Encyclopedia on subjects, such as bridge, with which he was thoroughly unfamiliar. In 1956, Ted became the midwest correspondent for Sports Illustrated, a position which gave full expression to his talents and love for sports and writing for the next 25 years. His most widely remembered by line, "The last time around with Stan," was based on his travels with baseball Hall-of-Famer, Stan Musial, during Musial's last visits to each of the National League cities. Ted retired from Sports Illustrated in 1981 after a severe injury to his left arm. Ted remained an active athlete from his college graduation to well into the 1980's. Declared ineligible as an amateur athlete for five years following his coaching experience at George Washington, he nevertheless became a nationally-ranked handball player, reaching the semi-finals of the national tournament in 1940. He would later be inducted into the Missouri State Handball Hall of Fame. He also actively maintained his tennis skills, even after the injury to his left arm, rarely losing even a set to experienced players who included movie star, Charlton Heston. As intense a competitor as he was in sports, he was equally gentle and patient as a counselor to aspiring writers. His home contained an extraordinary amalgamation of unpublished manuscripts, published books (over 15,000), trophies, and personal mementos. It was as well a gathering place for friends, acquaintances, and the curious who would come to hear Ted relive his recollections of a remarkable life. Ted was preceded in death by his wife, the former Emily Sophian, who died in 1994. They were married 58 years. His son, Theodore Morgan O'Leary, Jr. died at the age of 30 in 1971 in a small plane crash. He is survived by his son, Dennis S. O'Leary of St. Charles, IL., as well as six grandchildren and three great-grandchildren.

The home in which Emily and Ted lived for more than half a century passed to their only living son, Dennis S. O'Leary (one of the authors). The immediate task facing Dennis and his wife Margaret (the other author) was to safeguard the house from falling down and rescue its historic contents.

While cleaning the house, we found a remarkable and fairly complete set of letters and other written materials relating to Emily's Wohelo camp experience in the summer of 1928. We cleaned and sorted them and compiled the present biography/autobiography that focuses on a specific time of Emily's life. Hiiteni believed that the girls who attended Wohelo were going to be "the leading women of the future." In the case of Emily Sophian O'Leary, Hiiteni was correct.

Emily's letters and short pieces are reproduced verbatim (i.e., word for word, without corrected spellings, word usage, or grammar) and without redaction so that Emily and the people with whom she corresponded may speak directly to you and to the historical record.

We thank Louise Van Winkle and Mark Van Winkle, granddaughter and great-grandson, respectively, of Charlotte and Luther Gulick of Wohelo camp, who have been gracious in permitting publication of historic photos from their archives and generous in providing us with additional materials.

As authors, we want this book's treatment of Wohelo camp and of Emily Sophian's Wohelo camp experience to be fair and accurate, and would be pleased to correct any identified errors of fact. If an error of fact is identified, please contact the publisher who will forward your message to us for prompt consideration of text revision.

Margaret R. O'Leary, MD
Dennis S. O'Leary, MD
Fairway, Kansas
June 1, 2011

Emily Sophian, 1928

CHAPTER ONE:

Emily Sophian's Early Life, 1913–1928

Emily Sophian was born on September 28, 1913 to Estelle Felix (1886–1970) and Abraham Sophian (SO-fee-yun) (1884–1957) in the Hospital for Women at 19 West 101st Street, New York City.[1] She was their first child.

Estelle and Abraham Sophian were the youngest children of two immigrant families from the Russian Empire. Estelle was born in New York City and Abraham in Kiev. The Felix and Sophian families were part of the first wave of Eastern European immigration to the United States triggered by the Russian Empire's anti-Jewish pogroms of 1881–1884. The Felix and Sophian families arrived in 1883 and 1890, respectively. The two families escaped the deadly second and third waves of Eastern European pogroms (1903–1906 and 1919–1921), because they had moved to America to dwell in safety.[2–3] The Felix and Sophian families were of Greek and Armenian heritage, respectively.

Estelle and Abraham attended New York City public schools during the late 1800s. Estelle became a schoolteacher in the New York City public school system. Abraham attended Cornell University Medical College (1902–1906)[4–5], completed a two-year residency at Mount Sinai Hospital in New York City (1906–1908)[6], and then joined the Research Laboratory staff of the New York City Health Department (1908–1912).[7] He worked alongside physician-researchers William Hallock Park (director), Josephine B. Neal, and Phebe L. DuBois to develop and manufacture immune sera for the treatment of patients with infectious diseases in the pre-antibiotic era. Dr. Sophian

1

directed the Meningitis Division of the Research Laboratory and in late 1911 and early 1912 played a critical role in the successful efforts of Texas physicians in battling a widespread cerebrospinal meningitis epidemic.[8–10]

Abraham and Estelle married in 1911, had Emily in 1913, bore Abraham "Bud" Sophian, Jr. in 1915, and struck out for Kansas City, Missouri in 1917. They lived for twelve years in a beautiful apartment in Georgian Court built by Harry J. Sophian, Abraham's older brother, who was married to Jane Felix, Estelle's older sister.[11–13] Dr. Sophian was the first director of the medical laboratory (Research Laboratory) of Research Hospital (previously German Hospital and German-American) in Kansas City.[14] He opened a medical practice that thrived in Kansas City for more than thirty years. In the late 1920s and early 1930s, he helped raise private funding to build Menorah Hospital in Kansas City. Two of his most famous patients were Gilded Age lumber baron and city father Robert Alexander Long (1850–1934) and Kansas City Democratic boss Tom Pendergast (1873–1945).[15–16] The Abraham Sophian and Harry Sophian families witnessed but were not harmed by the 1918 influenza pandemic.[17–19]

By September 1918 Emily was old enough to start school. However, few options other than public school education existed for her, because secular private schools in Kansas City, i.e., Barstow School (founded 1884), Country Day School (founded 1910), and Sunset School (founded 1913) at the time refused admission to children of the Jewish faith. Estelle enrolled Emily in the all-girls French Academy (known later as the French Institute), which was founded and run by the sisters of Notre Dame de Sion, Kansas City. Estelle's sister Jane had sent her own daughter Lucile (also spelled Lucille; Emily's first cousin) (1909–1962) to the school beginning in 1916, and was pleased with the education Lucile was receiving.

The Congregation of Notre Dame de Sion was founded in 1843 by Théodore Ratisbonne (1802–1884), a scion of two wealthy Jewish families (Cerf Berr and Ratisbonne) of Strasbourg, Alsace. Théodore converted to Roman Catholicism in his twenties after a long period of inner conflict and study, entered the priesthood, moved to Paris, and became an assistant priest at Our Lady of Victories Church and the chaplain of an orphanage run by the Sisters of Charity. He also opened a small home for poor Jewish girls to demonstrate the "compassionate love of Jesus for the House of Israel, and His longing to draw the Jews to himself and convert them."[20–21]

On January 15, 1847, Pope Pius IX, the longest reigning elected pope in history (served 1846–1878), approved Ratisbonne's Paris community under the title chosen by Father Théodore: "La Congregation de Notre Dame de Sion." The Congregation of Notre Dame de Sion spawned dozens of convents with attached boarding schools in cities around the world, including Constantinople, Turkey (founded in 1856); "Ecce Homo," Jerusalem, Jordan (1859); "Ein Karem," Israel (1860); Baywater, England (1861); Worthing, England (1862); Cadi-keuy, Turkey (1863); Iassy, Roumania and Galatz, Roumania (1866); Marseille, France (1869); Holloway, England and St. Omer, France (1870).[22]

The sisters of Notre Dame de Sion first came to America in 1892 to teach in Lewiston, Maine, about twenty miles northeast of Sebago Lake and Wohelo camp. They made their way to Kansas City in 1911 where they established a convent and Emily's school, the French Academy, as noted above.[22] Emily recalled (at age fourteen years) her first days as a kindergartener at the French Academy, as follows:

> The memory of the day when I was first told that I was soon to begin my school career comes clearly back to me. I distinctly remember my indignation and my solemn vows that I should never be forced to attend such a place of horror, for, in my mind, that was what a school was. To my anger and disgust, however, mother paid no heed to my many tearful objections and made the necessary preparations.
>
> When the day of the opening of classes after the summer vacation arrived, it found a very peeved and disgruntled child being hurried into an already much despised uniform, for was it not the symbol of the terrible place she was being compelled to attend? Being very stubborn, however, I had not yet given up all hope of remaining in the home where I had been having so many good times, and a few minutes before eighty-thirty, the time classes were to begin, found a nearly distracted mother pleading vainly with a delighted child who had locked herself in the bathroom and who positively refused to come out. It took an hour's coaxing and the only whipping I ever received—(but what a whipping!)—to get a small tearstained, and rebellious girl into Mère Ida's classroom by a quarter of ten. But once there, all the animosity I bore my mother vanished and I clutched her hand in desperation, taking refuge behind her back from a black robed creature, whom I took to be one of the witches my aunts used to tell me about, and who tried to make me say a weird word,

(bonjour), which I was sure was some magic charm or other and which I firmly refused to repeat after her.

I was then introduced to some little girls of my age and while I was trying to decide whether or not I should speak to them, my mother slipped away. When I became aware of her disappearance, I set up a howl that successfully disturbed Mère Ida's class for the morning, for neither threats nor promises could make me hush. I wanted my mother, and they were finally forced to ask her to take her terrible daughter home to recuperate from her disastrous first day at Sion.

One year later, in 1919, the Abraham Sophian family joined Congregation B'nai Jehudah in Kansas City, which was fully modern in the Reform Jewish sense, e.g., services were in English, the rabbi's sermon was the main feature of the service, and families sat together in pews. Emily attended "Sunday School," later renamed "Religious School," at Temple B'nai Jehudah (1919–1928) and was confirmed into the adult community in 1927, one year before she attended Wohelo camp.[23-24]

In 1921, eight-year-old Emily met French Marshal Ferdinand Foch (1851–1929), supreme commander of the Allied armies during World War I, who paid a visit to Notre Dame de Sion (NDS). He told the students of Notre Dame de Sion that he loved France and he loved America, because they were truly like sisters, with deep ties of friendship. To assure this friendship, he noted, "The men fight—the women pray. Do not forget that it is your duty to pray."[22]

In 1921, Estelle enrolled Emily in a Kansas City dance school about which Emily wrote five years later in her short piece titled, "Ten Terrible Minutes."

> At the age of eight, although I had been attending dancing school for over a year, my movements were so awkward that I was the despair of my mother and teacher. Mother even had me take a few private lessons with the hope of somewhat improving my dancing (if my stumbling could so be termed), so that I would not cut too terrible a figure at the recital which was to take place at the Shubert [Theater] at the end of the year. Those lessons did little, if any, good, so that you can imagine my distress as the big (?) day drew near.
>
> My dancing class practiced at the Shubert several times a

week, and at each rehearsal I seemed to do worse. It certainly did not make me any happier when I compared myself with some of my friends who skipped and danced gracefully through the steps which I hated and which had become regular nightmares for me.

The day of the recital dawned at last. I believe that it was then that I first seriously contemplated running away—and I contemplated it very seriously indeed. Needless to say, however, "I did not choose to run." Nevertheless, if it had not been for my costume, which I found extremely fascinating, and which I was anxious to show off, I think I should have burst into tears as the orchestra struck up the opening notes of the piece to which I, together with several other girls, was to dance during the next few minutes. As it was, I turned red, stumbled, and had to be pulled out by my partner to skip miserably around the stage with my eyes glued on the floor. My mother must have been proud of me! Of the ghastly ten minutes which followed, I remember nothing except that a very unhappy, self-conscious little girl, sure that she was doing everything wrong, and that the whole audience was laughing at her, prayed to die harder than she had ever prayed for anything before.

It was over at last, but those few, terrible minutes marked the beginning and the end of my career as a dancer.

Emily was devoted to her younger brother Bud and described him as follows:

My brother was one of the prettiest babies I have ever seen. Not that I remember him very well as a baby, but he was really beautiful. However, shortly after the day he learned to walk, he developed into a regular little "family nuisance," as I term him. He has always taken the greatest delight in pestering both Mother and me – (Even Dad sometimes) – and, were it not for his charming disposition, I doubt very much if any nurse would have stayed with him over a week. As a child he was very much afraid of the water and much preferred playing in the sand to jumping in the pool or lake. In fact, it was not until just about a couple of years ago [when Bud was ten-years-old] that he overcame his fears and became a good swimmer. He now loves all water sports. However, he is a trouble-maker in the water as well as on land, for ducking people is one of his greatest sources of pleasure. I am almost certain that that is the reason mother cares so little for swimming.

From a beautiful, tho annoying child, Bud has grown into a handsome and still more annoying boy of twelve. He is extremely intelligent, although he does not work unless he has to, and is an excellent athlete, playing a very good game of tennis, golf and especially football. He should excel at the latter, however, for he practices his tackles on me at every available opportunity.

Now, in spite of his many attributes, especially his looks about which everyone comments, our "trouble-maker" remains naïve and not conceited. I think the world of him – (tho he does not seem to think I do) – and do not know how I'd ever get along without him.

Emily discovered pleasure and solace in writing and recalled the awakening of her love of writing in a short piece titled, "Oh, To Be an Authoress!" as follows:

As far back as I can remember, my greatest ambition and desire has been to write a book. In my early youth, the highly exciting "Bobbsey Twins" and "Ruth Fielding"[25-26] books filled me with "thrilling" plots of my own which I longed to put down on paper, but which I found difficult to express. In about the fourth grade I started a new "novel" every week, but after the first chapter or so was completed my ideas seemed to disperse, and, strange to say, I would lose interest, only to start on a fresh inspiration a few days later.

In the fifth grade I began my "masterpiece." It was "the thing," in our class at the time, to write stories, and no one was considered in style if there was not a mysterious little note-book peeping out of her uniform pocket. Most of the girls soon lost interest, but Justine and I remained faithful for almost a month. In our spare time we used to slide our "book" from our pockets and begin scribbling. I entitled mine "Kitty" and became deeply interested in it, having no idea at all about what I was going to have happen next. I do not know what Justine called hers, but, finally, even she weakened and I was left alone.

I continued filling "Kitty" with kidnappings, fires, floods, and all the other amazing and weird things of which I had read, endowing my heroine with the perfectness of Ruth Fielding and the resourcefulness of the Rover boys. But, alas, when my note-book was not quite half full, my interest waned and I put my "work of art" away for a year. When I was in the sixth grade I found it and recommenced work on it, writing whenever I had a chance. My family was quite proud of me (none of them except dad had read it) and often spoke of the high hopes they had for my future.

At last, that summer, amid many sighs of relief, I came to the last page of my note-book, consequently finishing my story. I at once wished to send it to be published, but, for some unknown reasons, my family was opposed and I was finally dissuaded. I put my "masterpiece" away and forgot it for a couple of years. This fall I found it and re-read it. I then realized why my family did not wish me to attempt to have it published.

During these last two years, I have started many stories with plots about which I knew next to nothing and never got very far with them. Nevertheless, in spite of all the silly ones I have written thus far, I hope some day to have some really worth while ones to my credit.

Before air conditioners became commercially available in the mid-1920s, Kansas City summers were hot and uncomfortable, sending affluent families packing for their summer cottages in the cooler climes of the northern United States. Dr. Sophian purchased a cottage for his family in Wildwood near Walloon Lake, north of Boyne City in the northwestern part of Michigan's Lower Peninsula. Emily spent summers at Walloon Lake beginning when she was seven years old (1921). She later recalled her experiences at Wildwood:

Placed between the blue waters of Walloon Lake, and the green, stately pines which compose the Michigan forests is a small summer colony bearing the name of Wildwood Harbor. The cottages, more or less far apart, are owned or rented mostly by resorters from Tulsa, Oklahoma, or Kansas City, MO. It is in this place that I have passed my last six summers.

The second year we went up there, Dad bought what I think is one of the most Attractive [sic] cottages on the lake, He had a clearing made in the back of the house for a baseball diamond for Bud and me; bought us a rowboat with a Johnson "putt-putt"; and last, but by no means least, had a canoe sent up to the lake from Chicago for us. Bud and I then settled down to make friends and enjoy ourselves. We were successful in doing both.

Bud got the boys, his own age and older and I met the girls.

The result was "the gang"—a group composed of about six boys and three girls with nothing to do but have a good time—and they did! Early almost every morning, the "war cry" which we used to summon each other, woke the resorters, and informed them that our round of hikes, ball games, swimming races, canoe races, and motor or sail boat rides, ending usually with a marshmallow roast and dance around ten or eleven P.M., had begun. If any of these things ever became tiresome for us, we always had a trip to Charlevoix, Petoskey, or Harbor Point, for a visit to the movies to fall back on.

Wildwood is like many other little resorts all over Michigan, Maine, Wisconsin, and many other states. One can have lots of fun in any of those places, but altho I hope to visit several of them besides the one on Walloon Lake, I doubt if I shall enjoy myself at any of them a bit more, if as much, as I did during my summers spent in Wildwood.

Emily wrote another short piece titled "The Biter Bitten" in which she describes one of her wilder summer escapades at Wildwood:

Anyone having lived on a farm or having visited one for any length of time has probably taken part in or been a spectator at an apple fight. Although I have never been on a farm except when I was quite young, about a quarter of a mile away from our cottage in Michigan, there is a farm in the hayloft of which my first attempt at apple fighting took place. I can hardly call it an attempt, for I was right in the thick of the battle all the time, and it was not a friendly one at that. If you have ever taken part in one like this, you will perhaps realize how desperate the situation became when, trapped in the loft by several farmer boys, we girls ran out of apples. "We" refers to some of my friends and myself who had gone into the barn to try to get hay fever by burying ourselves in the hay; who were trying to break our necks by falling through unexpected trap doors; and who had engaged in what began by being a friendly combat with the farmer boys and girls who owned the place, but which soon turned into a serious conflict with a great deal of bad feeling on both sides.

They soon began to jeeringly call us "ten cent millionaires" while we informed them that they were "country bumpkins". This exchange of "friendly" names succeeded in making our position extremely precarious, for it was just about then that the disheartening event mentioned happened, because, unless we had ammunition with which to guard our descent, we had no choice as to what to do; we would be forced to spend the rest of the afternoon (at least two hours) lodged in the loft. As you can imagine, this proposition did not highly appeal to our sense of humor, and we retired to a corner to hold a council of war. The "enemy", after firing one or two more apples, realized our predicament, ceased bombarding us, and, standing carelessly out in the open, laughed mockingly at our plight—a thing which did not lessen our discomfiture. I finally decided on a plan of campaign which, though you may think it foolhardy, seemed heroic to me. I decided to "sacrifice myself for the cause". Accordingly, I placed myself right in the opening, and posed as a target for the hail of nice, hard, green apples which immediately followed. I was kept quite busy, during the next few minutes, ducking around while my friends picked up the "ammunition". This state of affairs lasted for about five minutes. At the end of that time, my companions decided that they had enough apples to guarantee a comparatively safe descent and told me to come back in a corner. The summons came too late! Just at that moment a big, solid apple hit me square in the eye. Peace was declared at once.

I thought myself blinded, and wasn't feeling at all heroic when our erstwhile foes hurried up into the loft to see if I was hurt as badly as I thought I was. They sheepishly apoligized [*sic*], informed me that I was an utter fool but that I did have nerve, and that I had their permission to go home. I meekly accepted my dismissal, and, a few minutes later, headed for home with a rapidly swelling eye and some friends who were vying with each other to see which one of them could say "I told you so" loudest. Not a very heroic or triumphant return, was it?

In mid-September 1926, almost thirteen-year-old Emily, now in her eighth year at the French Academy, entered her freshman year of high school. Emily was growing tall, like her father, but was still shy of attaining her adult height of five feet and eight inches. The sisters of Notre Dame de Sion encouraged participation in sports, and Emily played on the school basketball team continuously from sixth to the twelfth grades (1924–1930). As a seventh and eighth grader, Emily watched the Sion high school girls play basketball. Their sweaters, with their patches carefully sewn on, inspired her to try to earn her own sweater and patches. Her short piece, titled "Winning and Decorating my Sweater," described her plan:

It was "Crawford's" [Ruth Crawford] decorated sweater that inspired me, when still a Sub [-Freshman], to try to win one something like it. I inquired about the system of points, tho I did not understand much of what I was told, and attended the Saturday morning basket-ball practices regularly. I knew that I did not stand a chance of making the team that season [as an eighth grader], but my hopes of getting on it in my Freshman year ran high. I do not think I won more than about eight points that year: five for being on the class team, and three for hiking. It was a poor beginning, but I was not discouraged.

The fall of 1926 saw a hopeful Freshman with only four points (those won during my Sub year were divided) determined to win her sweater and shield [a patch embroidered with the initials of Notre Dame de Sion]. This year my efforts were not in vain. After many hard practices, I finally made the squad, thereby winning my sweater and ten points. Tennis, hiking, and class teams gave me forty-six points by field-day. Though only four points were lacking, my last chance of obtaining my shield that year was gone unless I could win something in the track events. The end of the meet, after the ribbons and letters had been awarded, found me the happiest girl in the Freshman class, for I had not only received my much desired shield, but had also been given a basket-ball stripe for playing in over half the games. My one and only regret was that I had so little time left before the closing of school in which to exhibit the sweater of which I was so proud.

As a Sophomore, The [*sic*] desired goal is an N. D. S. [monogram]. That will mean fifty more points, and my hopes of obtaining it this year are not very high. Making the squad again gave me fifteen to begin on, plus five for class team. I cannot count on ten for hiking this year, however, because twenty instead of ten miles to a point make them <u>slightly</u> harder to earn.

I hope, nevertheless, to attain my N. D. S., if not while still a Soph, at least during my Junior year, so that, by the time I graduate, my sweater may somewhat resemble that of "Crawford," the girl I admire so highly.

Emily described the importance of the basketball experience at Sion in spring 1928, as follows:

Where would Sion be without basketball? Some might think

that a foolish and impolite question, but to me it seems perfectly natural. Not that I do not care for the school–I love it, but I am afraid that, were we deprived of the outside rivalry, and the relationship with other schools that basketball gives us, since we have not the sports and activities held in other schools, the girls would not like it here as well as they do. In my opinion, therefore, basketball is the last link in the chain of events which make of Sion one of the finest schools in the United States. This game, to-gether with the cheers and songs which accompany it, add the American touch to this otherwise very French school.

It is not only to Sion as a whole, however, that basketball has done good. It has also done "worlds" for the girls themselves, especially those on the squad to whom it has naturally meant more than it has to others. School spirit, good sportsmanship, loyalty, willingness to accept a reprimand cheerfully–those are only a few of the qualities that I think should be found in a girl who really takes this game seriously, who is willing to sacrifice for it, and who really loves it. All these qualities can be found, I think, in our captains of 1927 and 1928, and in the other four seniors who were on the team this year. Being on the squad, I got to know these girls well, and have learned to admire them all greatly. "Crawford," our captain of '27, led the way, and Jean, captain of '28, aided mostly by the other seniors of the team carried on. By that I do not mean that our team was undefeated, that we were champions–quite the contrary–but I do doubt if, anywhere in Kansas City, there are any girls who have proved themselves better sports and more loyal to their school than these have. The sisters and our teachers are, of course, responsible for this to a certain extent, but to basketball, the game which gave them a chance to fight for their school, and to show her how much she meant to them, a great deal of the credit is due.

Emily also described her perspective on the academic side of high school in her piece titled "Literature–English and French":

I have no favorite study–at least, there is no entire lesson that I like much better than any other. There is, however, one part of two of the subjects I take which I much prefer to anything else. That is–both English and French literature. I do not like the grammar of either at all, though I do like French verbs better than the English grammar rules.

Up to my "Sub-fresh" year, I do not know if the English books and stories we read in class could be called literature or not, but that year we took up what was to be my first narrative poem—[Sir Walter] Scott's [1771–1832] "Lay of the Last Minstrel." We also had some extracts from some of [Charles] Dickens' [1812–1870] works. This latter I did not particularly care for, but I liked the poem immensely.

In French that year we read "La Petite Princesse," a "sweet" story, but that is about all that can be said for it [by Henry Gréville, pen name for Mrs. Alice Durand (1842–1902)]. Last year we took the most interesting English course I have ever followed. It consisted of: [Sir Walter] Scott's "Lady of the Lake," [William] Shakespeare's [1564–1616] "Julius Caesar" and "Merchant of Venice," the "Autobiography of Benjamin Franklin" [1705–1790] (which I did not care for) and last, but not least, practically no grammar.

In French, my Freshman year, I do not think we took up any book in class, though we all did a great deal of outside reading, making monthly book reports.

This year [Sophomore] our English course thus far has been, with the exception of [Washington] Irving's [1783–1859] "Sketch Book [of Geoffrey Crayon]," based entirely on grammar, and while I feel as though I am learning a great many important things, English has not been quite so interesting for me. We have, however, several very good books to look forward to, and I am sure that I am going to like the last part of my Sophomore English better than the first.

In French, we have already read Moliere's [1622–1673] "Avare," [Pierre] Corneille's "Horace" [1606–1684] and are now taking "Athalie" by [Jean] Racine [1639–1699]. I like them all extremely well. I do not know exactly what my Junior and Senior English and French course will be, but I am sincerely hoping that we shall have exhausted the grammar of each by then, and will be able to have a course based almost entirely on literature.

In 1926, the new head of the convent, Notre Mère Irene, sailed from Paris to the United States on the *Rochambeau*, took the train to Kansas City, and replaced the retiring French Academy founder, Notre Mère Théotime. Notre Mère Irene took a special interest in Emily, whom she cherished as a daughter.

In 1927 Emily contemplated her future in an essay titled "Miss?":

Interrogatives, and then some more question marks! That is the present state of my mind concerning my future vocation. During the past two years, I have decided on a new one at the rate of at least one a month, and have not yet come to a decision. Dad would like to have me study medicine, so when I speak to him about it, I am absolutely certain that I will be nothing but a baby doctor.

Ten minutes after my "positive" decision has been made, mother tells me of the hard life a doctor leads, how nerve-racking it is, and, in other words, does her best to discourage me. By the time she has finished, I am thoroughly convinced that I was not cut out to be a physician, and decide, instead, to be an authoress as she would like me to be (even though I can't write).

I therefore discard the medical profession until I return to school. There I discover, to my dismay, that some of the girls I like best are thinking of studying medicine. I soon revert to my first decision, and even choose the college (I have picked three so far) at which I intend to study.

I generally remain a "doctor" for a few weeks, then one evening, my uncle [Harry] or aunt [Jane] will happen to start discussing what my brother and I shall probably do when we finish school. As soon as I mention medicine in a firm and convincing tone, they all laugh at me, and, after a short time my convincing manner is changed for a wavering, defensive one. In fact, to quiet them, at times I have decided to be either a clerk or a secretary, and if they were displeased by those, I "gently" reminded them that the salesgirl profession was open to whomever wished to try her hand at it. I say that I think it would be a lot of fun to stand behind a counter and chew gum all day long—and they believe me!

By then, mother, really dismayed, tells me that my aspirations are too lofty, so, to please her, the other day I decided that I would simply love to be a "gym" teacher, such as Miss Morrison [physical education teacher at Notre Dame de Sion], for there is quite a difference between that occupation and the ones mentioned in the preceding paragraph. Mother merely laughed, but for once I was serious. I think that I should really like it, because I love all sports.

To tell the truth, however, I don't think there is much hope for me along that line, because, with Mother and her literary ambitions for me on one side, and Dad and his medical ones on the other, I am afraid that I shall end up in a hospital after all—either as a doctor or as a patient.

In another short piece, Emily related her feelings about her future in, "What I am Doing with My Life," as follows:

Until this year, my main idea was to have a good time, to have as much fun as I possibly could, and I haven't, consequently, taken anything really seriously. This year, for the first time, I have tried to think of the future, tried to decide something definite about my future. I want to go through college, but if I study medicine, as I very probably shall, I think that I should study as little as possible at college, and enjoy myself as much as I could there, since in medical college it would be all grind and really no fun. Perhaps that is the wrong idea. Some people might say: "If you only want fun, why go to college?" My reasons are these: College has always been something vague and indefinite for me – I want to know what it is, what college life really means; and besides, if I study medicine, I shall need some kind of an academic college background. If I didn't want to follow a career, if I could count on the days of "doing nothing" that would follow my college graduation, perhaps I would take it more seriously. But I dread the thought of "doing nothing," of "playing" all the time. Why it wouldn't even be fun, it wouldn't be interesting anymore, and I think it would grow monotonous, tiresome! I think almost any girl gets tired of a continual, unceasing round of amusement if there is nothing more solid to look forward to – I know that I should. Most girls, in spite of the fact that they like their schools, much prefer vacations to classes; yet would they look forward to these vacations with so much pleasure if their life was one continued holiday? I think not – it's the work that makes us appreciate the "play." By this, however, don't think that, when I finish school, I intend to spend all my time laboring away at medicine, if I follow that career, so that I can enjoy more fully a spare moment snatched away every now and then. Not at all! But I do want to have a career firmly enough established to feel that I am not wasting my life away "having a good time."

During spring 1928, Estelle Sophian registered Emily for Wohelo, an all-girls, campfire-themed summer camp on Sebago Lake in southern Maine. Mrs. Sophian also registered Bud for Timanous, an all-boys' camp on Panther

Pond some eight miles north of Wohelo. Emily and Bud attended the seven-week summer session at the two camps from Friday, July 1, 1928, to Friday, August 26, 1928. South Casco, Maine was twice as far from Kansas City as was Wildwood, 1,600 miles versus 850 miles.

Emily and Abraham, Jr. (Bud) Sophian in their pram on a porch in Tulsa, Oklahoma, April 1916. Image credit: Sophian Archives, Fairway, Kansas.

15

Georgian Court Apartments, Kansas City, Missouri (Image taken in 2010). Image credit: M. O'Leary.

From left to right, Abraham (Bud) Sophian, Jr., Estelle
Sophian, and Emily Sophian, Kansas City, Missouri, 1919.
Image credit: Sophian Archives, Fairway, Kansas.

Notre Dame de Sion French Academy, in the old Kirk Armour mansion, Kansas City, Missouri (postcard). Image credit: Sophian Archives, Fairway, Kansas.

Emily and Abraham (Bud) Sophian, Jr., Walloon Lake, Wildwood, Michigan, summer 1922. Image credit: Sophian Archives, Fairway, Kansas.

Dr. Abraham Sophian (left) and his patients Robert Alexander Long (center) and Tom Pendergast (right). Kansas City, Missouri, circa 1925–1930. Image credit: Sophian Archives, Fairway, Kansas.

Notre Dame de Sion High School basketball team 1927. Emily
Sophian is third from the left. Captain Ruth Crawford is second from
the right. Image credit: Sophian Archives, Fairway, Kansas.

CHAPTER TWO:

Wohelo: Maine Setting and Founders

Wohelo camp is located on the west side of Raymond Neck (also called Raymond Cape), a stretch of billowy, cracked granite jutting southward about five miles into the main body of Sebago Lake, a freshwater inland body of water fed by springs, ponds, and streams.[1] Sebago Lake's maximum length, width, and surface area are approximately twelve miles, eight miles, and forty-six square miles, respectively. Its maximum depth is 316 feet, and its elevation is 272 feet above mean low tide in the harbor at Portland, Maine about twenty miles to the southeast.[2] Sebago Lake is the second largest lake (after Moosehead Lake) in the state of Maine. It originally formed at the southern edge of the North American continental ice sheet over 14,000 years ago.[3]

South Casco is the nearest town to Wohelo camp. *Casco* and *Sebago* are Indian names that mean "marshland" and "big stretch of water," respectively.[2] The Sokoki Native Americans, who belong to the Abenaki people (the original natives of New England), lived on Sebago Lake land for many centuries before European disease and fighting decimated their numbers between 1600 and 1800 AD.[4] South Casco became a favored destination for Emily and her Wohelo campmates.

Luther Halsey Gulick, Jr. (1865–1918) and his wife Lottie Emily Vetter Gulick (1865–1928) founded Wohelo camp in 1907. Lottie later changed her name to Charlotte. She was born in Oberlin, Ohio, on December 12, 1865, to Reverend John Vetter (1828–1912) and Ada Ann Rust (1825–1883).[5-6] Reverend Vetter was a native of Hersfeld, Hessen, Germany, who had immigrated to America at age three with his father in 1831. Ada Ann Rust was a native of Massachusetts. In 1859, John Vetter graduated from Oberlin College, which Presbyterian ministers John Jay Shipherd (1802–1844) and Philo P. Stewart (1798 – 1868) founded in 1833.[7–8]

In 1859, John and Ada married, and John then undertook further studies at Oberlin Graduate School of Theology, graduating in 1862.[9] Reverend Vetter served as chaplain at the end of the Civil War (March 1865–March 1866) for the Union Army's 5th Regiment of the US Colored Cavalry, a unit raised in Ohio and comprised of mostly free blacks who fought for the Union cause during the American Civil War.[10–12]

After discharge from the army, Reverend Vetter served as a home missionary with the American Home Missionary Society, which was formed in 1826 by the Congregational, Presbyterian, Dutch Reformed, and Associate Reformed Churches "with the purpose of financially assisting congregations on the American frontier until they could become self-sufficient." Reverend Vetter was the pastor at a number of Midwestern Congregational churches, meaning a Protestant Christian church that practices Congregationalist church governance (i.e., each congregation autonomously runs its own affairs). In 1863 Reverend Vetter formed a new church in Pent Water (Pentwater), Michigan on Lake Michigan's eastern shore, in 1870 he served as pastor of a church in Tontogany, Ohio, and from 1885–1904 he served as pastor in Eldon, Missouri.[13–15]

John and Ada Vetter had four children: Anna Maria (born 1860), Julia Christina (1862–1867), Lottie Emily, and Bertrand Elijah Vetter (1867–1878). Charlotte obtained her early formal education in Kansas public schools, and subsequently spent four years doing college preparatory work at Washburn College (founded in 1865 by a charter issued by the State of Kansas and the Association of Congregational Ministers and Churches of Kansas) in Topeka, Kansas, and Drury College (founded in 1873 by Congregational home missionaries) in Springfield, Missouri. She then formally matriculated at Drury College as a full-time college student and earned her bachelor of arts degree three years later.

In 1884 Charlotte Vetter and Luther Halsey Gulick, Jr. met at a Drury College "river party," during a camping trip, or both.[16] Three years later, on August 30, 1887, they married in Hanover, New Hampshire when both were twenty-one-years-old. They spent their honeymoon camping in Meredith, New Hampshire, beside Lake Winnipesaukee, the largest lake in New Hampshire. Lake Winnipesaukee is about fifty miles west of Sebago Lake in Maine.

Luther Halsey Gulick, Jr. came from a large multi-generational family of American foreign missionaries. He was born on December 4, 1865 in Honolulu, the Sandwich Islands (Hawaiian Islands). Captain James Cook (1728–1779) named them Sandwich Islands after his financial supporter, Englishman John Montagu (1718–1792), 4th Earl of Sandwich. Luther Gulick, Jr. was the fifth of seven children (Frances, Harriet, Sidney, Edward, Luther (Jr.), Orramel, and Pierre) born to Congregational missionary Luther Halsey Gulick, Sr. (1828–1891) and Louisa Mitchell Lewis (1830–1894). Luther Halsey Gulick, Sr. and Reverend John Vetter were born the same year (1828), just as Luther Halsey Gulick, Jr. and Charlotte Vetter were born in the same year (1865).

Luther Halsey Gulick, Sr. was born in the Sandwich Islands to missionary Peter Johnson Gulick (1796–1877) and Fanny Hinckley Gulick (1798–1883). Peter Johnson Gulick was the third of seven sons of a New Jersey farmer and a descendant of Hendrick Gulick, who immigrated to the United States from the Netherlands in 1653. Peter Johnson Gulick graduated from Princeton College in 1825, studied at and graduated from Princeton Theological Seminary, married Fanny Hinckley Thomas, and in November 1827 sailed with her from Boston, Massachusetts, under appointment as a missionary to the Hawaiian Islands and Micronesia.[17] The following March (1828), only eight years after the opening of the mission to the Hawaiian Islands, Peter and Fanny reached Honolulu by way of Cape Horn, the rugged southernmost tip of Chile.

Fanny and Peter Gulick had eight children. One died, but the other seven became missionaries. Their oldest son was Luther Halsey Gulick, Sr., mentioned above. In autumn 1841, at age thirteen, Luther Gulick, Sr. sailed from Honolulu, around Cape Horn to New York City, and thence to Auburn, New York, where he attended an academy. After further study with a physician in Amboy, New Jersey, he studied for three years at the College of Physicians and Surgeons (founded in 1807 by the New York State Board of Regents) and the medical department (founded 1841) of the University of New York, from which he earned his medical school diploma in 1850 at age twenty-two. The next year he was ordained a missionary. He then married Louisa Lewis, daughter of a New York merchant, and sailed around Cape Horn back to Honolulu. Fourteen years later (1865), Luther Halsey Gulick, Jr. entered the world.

The fathers of Luther, Jr. and Charlotte were both American Protestant Christian Congregational missionaries. However, Luther, Jr.'s father, grandfather, and many other relatives were *foreign* missionaries, while Charlotte's father was a *home* missionary.

As a youngster, Luther, Jr. traveled with his father and other members of his family on Congregationalist missionary work to Spain, Italy, and other European Roman Catholic countries. Luther Gulick, Sr. worked under the auspices of the American Board of Commissioners for Foreign Missions, which was chartered by graduates of Williams College, Williamstown, Massachusetts, in 1812. Its founding was associated with the Second Great Awakening.[18-20]

At age fifteen (1880), Luther Gulick, Jr. moved to Oberlin, Ohio, to live with his older sister, Sarah Frances Gulick Jewett (1854–1937) and her husband, Professor Frank Fanning Jewett (1844–1926) whom she had married in 1880.[21] Frank F. Jewett had earned baccalaureate and master's degrees at Yale College in New Haven, Connecticut in 1870 and 1873 and then relocated to Oberlin College upon his appointment as professor of chemistry and mineralogy, a position he held for the next forty years.[22-23]

During the years 1880–1882, Luther took classes at Oberlin Academy, which was the preparatory department of Oberlin College. His mother Louisa meanwhile had left Japan because of ill health to move to Hanover, New Hampshire to live with her two sons, Sidney (1860–1945) and Edward. The two young men were attending Dartmouth College from which they each earned their baccalaureate degrees in 1883.[21]

Luther, Jr. moved to Hanover to be with his mother and older brothers for the year 1882–1883, and while there he attended Hanover High School. He then returned to study at Oberlin Academy during the period 1883–1886, but did not complete high school or matriculate at Oberlin College. Instead, in 1886 he moved with a friend to Cambridge, Massachusetts to study physical education with Professor Dudley Allen Sargent, MD (1849–1924), founder and director of the Harvard University-affiliated Normal School of Physical Training. Dr. Sargent was also director of Harvard's Hemenway Gymnasium.[21,25-26]

Luther Gulick, Jr. studied with Dr. Sargent for less than a year before moving to Jackson, Michigan in the mid-1880s to work as the physical director of the city's Young Men's Christian Association (YMCA). The YMCA was founded in 1844 in London, England by Sir George Williams (1821–1905).[27] In 1851, Thomas Valentine Sullivan (1800–1859), a retired American sea captain and lay preacher, led a group of local churchmen to found the first YMCA in the United States in Boston, Massachusetts. Captain Sullivan had observed the work of the London YMCA and saw the association as an opportunity to provide a "home away from home" for young sailors on shore leave. "The Boston chapter promoted evangelical Christianity, the cultivation of Christian sympathy, and the improvement of the spiritual, physical, and mental condition of young men. By 1853, the Boston YMCA had 1,500 members, most of whom were merchants and artisans."[26] Thus the YMCA had been in existence for thirty-six years when Luther Gulick, Jr. began to work for the organization in Jackson, Michigan.

Luther Gulick, Jr. understood the need to acquire additional formal education and a valid diploma. On December 16, 1886, at age twenty-one years, he was accepted to New York University Medical College (the same medical college from which his father had graduated thirty-six years before) and happily earned his medical diploma in 1889. Historian Claude Edwin Heaton wrote in 1941 the following about New York University Medical College, which, he noted, had opportunity for improvement like many medical schools of the era:

> Between 1841 and 1897, the [New York] University Medical College was in reality a proprietary school although under nominal university control. Standards had sunk to a very low level. In the year 1895–1896, the State Regents placed the University Medical College lowest of the twelve schools whose graduates they examined for license to practise [sic] in the State of New York. The main difficulty was dissension among the faculty. University control was urgently needed, so on March 1, 1897, the Council assumed direct charge of the Medical College.[28]

For the six weeks of July and August 1887, Luther Gulick, Jr. and Robert J. Roberts (1849–1920) moved to Springfield, Massachusetts to conduct the first summer school for directors of YMCA gymnasia. The Springfield YMCA was then a department of the School for Christian Workers, which itself was founded in 1885 by Congregational Reverend David Allen Reed (1850–1932) to prepare, over the course of two years, young men for Christian work as Sunday school superintendents, secretaries of the YMCA, pastors, lay assistants, and Bible colporteurs and readers. The education also prepared Christian men for lay home mission work.[29]

Robert J. Roberts had obtained his early physical education training in the proprietary gymnasiums in Boston and had served as a physical director of the Boston YMCA. Gulick and Roberts clashed while employed at Springfield. One historian noted:

> It was almost inevitable that these two gentlemen would soon be at cross-purposes in the light of their divergent social and educational backgrounds. Roberts's program of hygienic body building was simple, mechanical, and readily taught to the masses. Under contemporary conditions his program of health-building exercises as "safe, short, easy, beneficial and pleasing" undeniably fulfilled a felt need but was not fully appreciated by Gulick. The breach became so wide that Dean Seerley ... candidly admitted "they agreed on nothing."[30]

> Gulick could not conceive of physical education as a predetermined set of artificial movements and dumbbell drills. He envisioned his mission at the School for Christian Workers to be the development of a program that would be creative, progressive, and experimental in its approach. In this role he set out "to investigate the subject, open up new fields, devise new methods and improve the old."[30]

Roberts resigned his position in Springfield two years later, because of his unwillingness to teach some of the more advanced types of educational and recreational gymnastics.[30]

In September 1887, Luther Gulick, Jr. was promoted to supervise the "physical side" of YMCA in the entire United States, even as he attended medical school classes in New York City. Indeed, Luther served (1887–1888) as medical examiner of New York City's Twenty-third Street YMCA (where the famous professional oarsman William Wood [1815–1900] was still superintendent of the gymnasium) and even oversaw physical education at a girls' school in Harlem. The money Luther Gulick, Jr. earned in these positions helped pay for his medical education.[21]

The same year Luther began work at the YMCA school in Springfield, Massachusetts, he married Charlotte Vetter, as noted above, who spent a year of pre-medical studies at Wellesley College (Wellesley, Massachusetts) and a year accompanying her new husband to medical school classes in New York City, "the better to assist him in the mission field which he was then planning to enter, following his father's precedent."[31]

However, the couple's life took a decidedly different turn, and they did not become either home or foreign missionaries. Charlotte "convinced Luther to remain in the United States as she believed he had much more to contribute to the children of his own country in the field of physical education than he would if he traveled abroad," noted her daughter Charlotte Gulick Hewson.[32] Charlotte understood her husband's gift as a potential physical education philosopher who could "forge physical culture to Christian philosophy."[33]

In 1890 leaders of the Springfield YMCA "found it necessary for its welfare and progress [to] resign its position as a branch of the School for Christian Workers" to become "an independent organization under its present name," i.e., Young Men's Christian Association Training School.[34] The YMCA training school would undergo several more name changes, i.e., International YMCA Training School, International YMCA College, and, in 1954, Springfield College, the name it retains today.[35]

The two major buildings on the Springfield YMCA campus in the 1880s were the men's dormitory and the school's hallowed gymnasium. In 1891 Dr. Gulick challenged his instructors to develop an indoor game that "would be interesting, easy to learn, and easy to play in the winter and by artificial light." Canadian native Dr. James Naismith (1861–1939), an instructor who responded to that challenge, recalled in 1902:

> About this time there was a protest against the introduction of Swedish educational gymnastics to take the place of the children's recess in the public schools. This led to a question of games. At a meeting of the physical department held at Dr. Gulick's house [in Springfield, Massachusetts] the point was brought up as to what constitutes a good game, and it was agreed that so far as the development of the right kind of manhood was concerned, lacrosse was the ideal game. I tried all the games that seemed to offer any hope and studied each carefully, but kept the idea of lacrosse always in mind. Then it occurred to me that the only way was to get one that would fill the requirements as nearly as possible.
>
> That there should be a ball of some kind was the point to be settled upon, because by this means the game could be made scientific and interesting, bringing in the element of physical judgment and yet be free from the personal contact which is so often the cause of roughness. A large ball was used in order that it might be handled with the hands and not hidden, and besides it

required no practicing with a stick or bat. The next question was to prevent roughness. In order to eliminate the tackling feature of football the person holding the ball was not allowed to run with it, but was required to throw it from the place in which he caught it, thus doing away with the necessity for tackling. To obviate the roughness sometimes prevalent in association with football in kicking the ball it was made contrary to basket ball rules to kick the ball. The players were also prevented from using their fists in striking the ball, and all personal contact was absolutely forbidden.

In all games where the opening of the goals is vertical, there is a great deal of swift passing and throwing, which in a gymnasium would ultimately result in damage to the apparatus and possibly to the players. To overcome this in an indoor game the goals were placed horizontally and at such a height that a player could not cover them and prevent the entrance of the ball. The first goals were simply a couple of peach baskets hung at each end of the gymnasium and hence the game took its name. Basket ball was thus made in the office, and was a direct adaptation of certain means to accomplish certain ends. The rules were formulated before the game was ever played by any one, in fact, they were typewritten and hung up in the gymnasium before the game was started, so that all the training school members might know just what to do. Of course there was some doubt as to the success of the venture, but only a few trials were needed to demonstrate its popularity, and from that moment its growth has been rapid.[36]

Thus the game of basketball was invented in 1892. Historian Elmer Johnson wrote:

The game swept the country by storm and was soon played from Maine to California and from Michigan to Texas. The first YMCA to adopt the game outside Springfield was the Providence, Rhode Island Association. The first colleges outside of Springfield to adopt the game were Geneva College at Beaver Falls, Pennsylvania, and the University of Iowa.[37]

A *New York Times* article dated December 23, 1902 elaborated on the popularity of basketball, as follows:

Hundreds of young men are now playing basket ball who probably have but a vague idea regarding its origin or realize that for so young a sport it has had a most unusual career. Started first as a game for members of the gymnasium classes of Young Men's Christian Associations, it has now attracted the attention of all classes of athletes, as is seen from the scores of associations that now exist, including intercollegiate, interscholastic, Christian Association, and even professional. So prominent has it become that the Amateur Athletic Union has added basket ball to its list of sports for legislation on an amateur basis, and the number of suspended teams recently made in this and other local associations shows how rigorously the Amateur Athletic Union is keeping watch over this phase of athletic amusement.

Basketball had its birthday in Springfield, Mass., eleven years ago. Dr. James Naismith has been given the unquestioned honor of inventing it, for it was an invention pure and simple. Unlike baseball, football, hockey, golf, and other sports, it was not evolved into its present standard through years of growth with gradual improvements, but leaped with one bound into its present position. The method of playing the game to-day and its rules differ only in the merest details from the first games played eleven years ago.

Dr. James Naismith brought out the game while he was an instructor in the Young Men's Christian Association training school in Springfield. Dr. Luther Gulick, who is now in Brooklyn, was also an instructor in the school at the same time, and he had a share in bringing the game to perfection. He has always maintained an unflagging interest in the sport, and is the Chairman of the Basket Ball Committee of the Amateur Athletic Union.

In March 1893, Senda Berenson (1868–1954), director of physical culture at Smith College (founded 1871) in Northampton, Massachusetts, first introduced basketball to women after visiting Dr. Naismith in nearby Springfield to understand the new game.[38] One Smith College player described that first game between representatives of the freshmen and sophomore classes:

Friday afternoon at the Gym, we played a game, instead of going through the ordinary performances. Two wastepaper baskets were hung, one on either side of the Gym, about three feet above our heads. Two of the girls chose sides, and those on our side were distinguished from the other by handkerchiefs tied on their arms.

31

Three girls from each side were sent over to the other and the game began. We had a football which was to be touched only with the hands, and the object was to get it into your opponent's basket and keep it out of your own. ... It was great fun and very exciting, especially when we got knocked down, as frequently happened."[38]

Berenson worried, "The great danger of the game is its tendency to roughness." Indeed, one girl dislocated her shoulder at the ball toss, but it was quickly relocated. However, Berenson reminded herself, "Must remember this was the first team sport girls every played" and noted, "From the first, the winning team gave a dinner to the defeated team. Girls sat together who had played against each other, and speeches of good will were made by the captains and the gym faculty—and I was proud of the spirit of those girls."[38]

In 1892, eleven months after Berenson introduced basketball at Smith College, the first official women's basketball game between two institutions took place between a group of women at the University of California at Berkeley and Anna Head's School, a girls' college preparatory school (founded 1887) then at 2538 Channing Way in Berkeley. By 1893, the women of Mt. Holyoke College (South Hadley, Massachusetts) and Sophie Newcomb Memorial College (New Orleans, Louisiana) had begun to play, and by 1895, the game was played all across the country, most prominently at Wellesley (Massachusetts), Vassar (New York) and Bryn Mawr (Pennsylvania) women's colleges. The rules depended on where it was played and committees met endlessly to discuss regulations, noted women's basketball historian Sally Jenkins.[38]

Berenson modified the basketball rules for girls, including dividing the court into three zones, with nine players on each team, equally divided among the zones. The girls could not leave their zones, could not grab the ball from another girl, and could not hold the ball for more than three seconds. Berenson's rules, first published in 1899, were approved by the American Association for the Advancement of Physical Education and were used until the 1960s. However, not all girls' basketball teams long followed these rules. For example, Emily's basketball team at Notre Dame de Sion switched from "girls rules" to "boys rules" in 1929.

Dr. Luther Gulick, Jr. and his mentor Dr. Dudley Sargent believed that basketball was too rough for girls or women. A *New York Times* article (March 31, 1906) titled "Perils that Women Find in Athletics; Dr. Sargent Warns

Them Against Emulating Men in Sports; Let Women Stick to Lighter and Graceful Forms of Exercise, Says Harvard's Physical Director" quoted their beliefs, as follows:

> According to opinions expressed by authorities who addressed the Public School Physical Training Society at a mass meeting held last evening at the hall of the Board of Education in Fifty-ninth Street, woman for her own good should not strive to emulate man in the more strenuous forms of athletics, particularly competitive games, and should pursue physical training merely for recreation and pleasure. …
>
> Dr. Dudley Sargent, Physical Director at Harvard University, was the principal speaker. He struck the keynote of the evening in a discussion of "What athletic games, if any are injurious for women in the form in which they are played by men?" Dr. Sargent said: "In physical education women should not be expected to excel in physical exercises which are adapted to men, nor should they be required to teach athletics to men and boys, as is the case in some of the schools in the West. Such a requirement is not only injurious to the women, but equally injurious to the men. Let woman rather confine herself to the lighter and more graceful forms of gymnastics and athletics, and make herself supreme along these lines as she has already done in aesthetic dancing. Let her know enough about the rougher sports to be the sympathetic admirer of men and boys in their efforts to be strong, vigorous, and heroic.
>
> While admiring and applauding all there is in athletics which tends to make boys courageous and manly, let her not hesitate to condemn all that tends to make them mean, vicious, and cowardly. Let woman use her influence in trying to raise football and some of the rougher athletic games from their barbaric stage to a standard more in keeping with our present civilization, and she will do more for the moral and physical welfare of herself and the community than she could possibly do by entering the arena as a competitor in these contests."
>
> The forms of gymnastics to which woman should confine herself Dr. Sargent classified thus: All forms of dancing, calisthenics, and light gymnastics, archery, lawn tennis, swimming, field hockey, lacrosse, spring running, bicycling, rowing, canoeing, golf, skating, fencing, and all gymnastic plays and games. … Among the athletic sports and games that would be likely to prove injurious to most

women, if played in the form in which they are played by men, Dr. Sargent particularly mentioned football, ice hockey, basket ball, boxing, pole vaulting, heavy gymnastics. These games prove injurious to women, he said, because of the limitations imposed upon her by her physical configuration, the tendency to become masculine in form and character if she tries to excel in masculine pursuits, and her inability to bear a prolonged mental and physical strain. Nevertheless, he declared these sports and games could be so modified as to meet the peculiar requirements of woman, with the result that all of them could be played by her with reasonable hope of physical, mental, and moral development.

In his discussion of "Athletics from a Biological Viewpoint," Dr. Luther H. Gulick, President of the society, struck substantially the same note as Dr. Sargent by saying: "I believe that athletics for women should be restricted to sport within the school; that it should be used for recreation and pleasure; that the strenuous training of teams tends to be damaging to both body and mind, and that public general competition emphasizes qualities that are, on the whole, unnecessary and undesirable in women. Let us then have athletics for recreation, but not for serious public competition."

In addition to his position as the first director of physical education in the New York City public school system, Dr. Luther H. Gulick was editor of *American Physical Education Review*; co-founder of the Public Schools Athletic League in New York City (for boys); the first president of the Playground Association; and, in the 1910s, director of child hygiene for the Russell Sage Foundation, founded by Mrs. Margaret Olivia Sage in 1907 for "the improvement of social and living conditions in the United States."[39] Luther Gulick, Jr. was also a member of the Organizing Committee of the Boy Scouts of America and with his wife (her idea) founded the iconic Campfire Girls (also, Camp Fire Girls) organization in 1910. Luther was president of the national organization for several years.[40–41]

Luther Gulick, Jr. was a prolific writer on physical training and contributing subjects, as listed in the fine bibliography prepared by his biographer, Ethel Josephine Dorgan.[42] Examples of Luther Gulick's books are *The Efficient Life* (Garden City, New York: Doubleday, Page & Company, 1907) and *The Gulick Hygiene Series* (Boston, Massachusetts: Ginn and Company, 1906–1909). Luther planned and edited the five books of *The Gulick Hygiene Series*. However, Frances Gulick Jewett (who still lived in Oberlin) penned four of the books and Charlotte wrote the second book of the series, titled *Emergencies*. Other Luther Gulick books are *The Healthful Art of Dancing* (Garden City, New York: Doubleday, Page & Company, 1910); *Medical Inspection of Schools* (with Leonard P. Ayres, co-author) (New York City, New York: Russell Sage Foundation, 1908); and *A Philosophy of Play* (published posthumously) (New York City, New York: Charles Scribner's Sons, 1920).

During the first twelve years of their marriage (1887–1899), Charlotte and Luther Gulick had six children—Louise (December 1888–June 1944), Frances Jewett (April 1891–November 1936), Charlotte (November 1892–February 1909), Katharine F. (born March 1895), Luther (1897–1897), and John Halsey (December 1899–September 1980), who went by the name Halsey. Louise was born in New York and the other five children were born in Springfield, Massachusetts.[43]

In the late 1880s, the Gulicks began to "camp" at Gales Ferry on the shore of the Thames River in Connecticut. "Camping" to the Gulicks meant a voluntary, pleasurable, spiritually and physically stimulating, and temporary outdoor activity for which they left their urban home to spend days and nights outdoors at a campsite cooking over an open fire, swimming and boating on a river or lake, and sleeping in tents or under the stars. The Gulicks were among the first American "campers." Camping became popular as a recreational activity among many Americans in the late nineteenth and early twentieth centuries.[44]

The Gulicks' camp at Gales Ferry grew larger and more organized over time as they "[g]radually gathered friends around them until there were ten or twelve families. Each family was its own unit. Guests were frequent. Sometimes there were as many as ninety in camp … All the men were active in leaders' work, professors in colleges, or the like, so that camp offered an ideal life—friendly, congenial, stimulating neighbors and the outdoors with its lure of wood and water." Luther led the camp in singing, gymnastics, swimming, boating, tennis, fishing, long talks, and bonfires. Each year the camp held a "panjandrum" or jamboree, which consisted of clambakes, games, and contests in the water.[45]

While camping at Gales Ferry during the summer of 1897, Luther, the six-month-old son of Charlotte and Luther, became ill. Luther and another camper, Dr. Frank N. Seerley (dean of the International YMCA Training School in Springfield, Massachusetts), took the infant out on a sailboat, "thinking to benefit him." A storm arose that pitched them about all night and required dragging the anchor to stay upright. The baby died, according to Dorgan's interview with Dr. Seerley in the early 1930s.[45]

In 1907, the Gulicks left off camping at Gales Ferry, and began camping instead at Sebago Lake, South Casco, Maine, not far from where Charlotte and Luther had honeymooned in 1887. They chose Sebago Lake in 1907 after visiting the area and the White Mountain Camp for boys that had been established there in 1905 by their friend, Dr. George L. Meylan, who was educated at Harvard College and New York University Medical College. Emily wrote about the thrill of the fireworks and the verbally expressive boy campers of White Mountain Camp. Various reasons given for the Gulicks' departure from Gales Ferry were that they had outgrown Gales Ferry; the population of New London, Connecticut was rapidly increasing; the railroad's coming to the area disturbed the peace of Gales Ferry; and Charlotte and Luther wanted to "keep [their] family together" for the summer months. Charlotte recalled:

> By the time the eldest of the five was twenty and the youngest nine, outsiders began to discover in the older children the value of their experience. They were in demand at summer camps, for they knew how to do things. So, to keep our family together, we had to start a camp of our own and face new problems. We wanted to have our children learn in camp various hand-crafts, that called for expert paid instructors, and we wanted, besides, to give them the human, social experience of entertaining a group of their friends, both projects beyond our means. So a plan for the sharing of expenses was formulated, and in this way Sebago-Wohelo was started.[46]

The Gulick family had a happy autumn in 1908 during which Charlotte, the third Gulick daughter, had built herself a tree house in which to sleep overlooking Sebago Lake.[46] In 1908, she saved her brother, Halsey, when he fell out of their father's boat. Their mother Charlotte wrote in her book *Emergencies* (noted above) the following:

> [Charlotte, Jr.] was a good swimmer, and when she heard the splash she did not hesitate an instant, but dived in beside him and brought him up so quickly that the little chap said afterwards, "I didn't even get my hair wet." It was over before either of them had time to get frightened. Every summer this girl [Charlotte, Jr.]

and her sisters [Louise, Frances, Katharine] practice rescuing each other and their companions just for sport.[47]

Sadly, before the 1909 season began, "lovely and talented" Charlotte died suddenly at the age of seventeen.[48] Dorgan, who obtained her information about Charlotte's death from Louise Gulick in 1934, wrote the following:

> In 1909 Charlotte, the third daughter of the family, died. By some she was considered the most gifted of the Gulick children. She was very dear to the Doctor [Gulick]. Talented, full of vivacity, and unchecked in the expression of her gifts, friends feel that Charlotte injured herself by the long hours devoted to dancing, coupled with the other activities in which she engaged, that an overworked heart and the too free outpouring of energy made her unable to cope with pneumonia which caused her death.[49]

However, in 1908 Louise Gulick wrote to her mother that Charlotte had "inflamatory rhumatism [sic] in her ankle" for which "Dr. Meylan [has] given her something to paint her ankle with. She had a fever of 102 yesterday."[50] Dr. Meylan's assessment suggests acute rheumatic fever, a sequel of an untreated Group A streptococcal throat infection. Antibiotics did not exist in 1908, so the dreaded acute rheumatic fever was untreatable and sometimes fatal. The disease strikes children between the ages of five and seventeen, and may cause sudden death through destructive changes to the heart valves, heart muscle, or both.[51]

After Charlotte's death, "The family had little heart for the camp but did invite three girls to share their family life and, at the last moment, accepted as a paying guest a fourth girl who was a convalescent in need of an outdoor summer."[41] In 1910, the Gulick family united to found a new, yet unnamed camp on Sebago Lake. Fourteen girls, not including the three surviving Gulick daughters (twenty-one-year-old Louise, nineteen-year-old Frances, and fifteen-year-old Kitty) attended the camp. Historians described that first year of the camp:

> Louise [Gulick], in starched white shirtwaist and with her long skirts brushing the high tops of her laced black shoes, escorted the New York City contingent up to Boston on the night boat of the old Fall River Line [a combination steamboat and railroad connection between New York City and Boston that operated 1847–1937]. Crossing the [Boston] harbor after breakfast the girls

scattered tea leaves and enjoyed their own Boston Tea Party. After a day's educational sight-seeing, another night-boat trip landed them in Portland. Then by train to [Sebago Lake] Station and [north] across Lake Sebago by steamer and launch to rock-bound WoHeLo where Halsey Gulick, "Helpful the Little," aged ten, greeted them with the bugle—or tried to. He had not yet learned how to put sufficient "blow" into the instrument without holding his nose ... It was quite a trick to gather up your handbag and your long full skirts and get out of the launch without getting wet ... A stiff climb up the rocks and they were welcomed by Mrs. Gulick ... Once out of their heavy skirts and into voluminous bloomers and middies, with long black stockings and white tennis shoes to complete the costume, life took on a new freedom. When they went swimming and canoeing they put on black bathing dresses with square necks and knee-length skirts and left off their stockings.[41]

In 1911, Mrs. Gulick officially consecrated the camp *Wohelo*, famously creating the word from the first two letters of three words: work, health, and love. Mrs. Gulick "believed that in constructive work lay the roots of true service to humanity and the real joy of living. Health was fundamental and Love was [the] highest law."[41] The name Sebago Wohelo distinguished the camp on Sebago Lake from other Wohelo namesake camps sprouting up across the United States as part of the explosive growth of the Camp Fire Girls movement during the first half of the twentieth century. The Gulick camp in Maine and the Camp Fire Girls movement were co-born from the vision and work of the Gulick family. "Just where the Gulick family experience stopped and the Gulick Camps and Camp Fire began it is difficult to say," observed Dorgan.[42]

In 1928, Wohelo accepted girls aged thirteen to eighteen years. A second camp called Little Wohelo, also on Sebago Lake and owned by the Gulicks, accepted girls aged eight to thirteen years. Camp Timanous accepted boys aged seven to fourteen years. When Dr. Gulick died on August 13, 1918, Charlotte changed the name of the three camps to the Luther Gulick Camps, in his memory. Membership in the Camp Fire Girls was not a prerequisite for attending Wohelo or Little Wohelo, and Emily was not a member of the Camp Fire Girls organization.

Charlotte Gulick understood the value of themes in organizing the camping experience and developed Wohelo around elements of "Indian" and "gypsy" cultures, both of which share the camp fire as a central element. She consulted her friend Ernest Thompson Seton (1860–1946) in formulating Wohelo's philosophy. Seton was a famed nature writer who founded the League of Woodcraft Indians, an American youth program.[52] Charlotte chose an Indian name for herself—"Hiiteni"—which means "life, more abundant and desire for attainment." She named her husband "Timanous," meaning "guiding spirit." Her daughter Louise named herself Pakwa (frog), Frances, Mahn-go-tay-see (fire maiden), and Kitty, Wa Wa (duck).[53]

As noted above, Luther Gulick grew up in a family filled with educated Protestant Congregationalist ministers and not surprisingly espoused the "creed of the [Christian] missionary" during his teaching and superintending days at the YMCA in Springfield, Massachusetts. Dorgan explained:

> At the time the physical education departments of the Young Men's Christian Associations were generally regarded as bait to draw young men into the religious departments. Few of the men who were in charge of the physical education departments were well educated or technically competent. Those few were usually non-Christians ... To [Luther Gulick, Jr.] it was unthinkable that a man of high ideals, character, education, and technical ability who did not profess Christ could be a suitable Association director. He used his influence to demand that each man in the service of the Association should be a Christian. He was also the first to promulgate the idea that a physical education director should have all the qualifications of a good teacher. The general attitude prevailed that if a physical education director became drunk it was to be deplored but nothing could be done about it. No serious-minded young man of sterling character could be expected to engage in such work.
>
> Dr. Gulick believed that there should be no conflict between the physical education and the religious departments. He thought that one was false to Christ to develop the religious side at the expense of either the physical or the mental phase, or both. Likewise he held that the physical or mental aspect or both should not be cultivated at the expense of the religious. He thought that great men are truly so only when there is symmetry in their development. ... He felt that physical law was divine law, that God did not call on one to do more than one's health would permit.[57]

Luther Gulick's early intense missionary outlook had evolved somewhat by the time he and Charlotte founded Wohelo and the Camp Fire Girls. Neither Christianity nor any other formal religious creed were an identifiable part of the Wohelo experience when Emily attended the camp in 1928. The Wohelo philosophy was to promote spiritual development and wholeness in an environment guided by the principles of work, health, and love. The religious policy of the Camp Fire Girls, as stated in 1948, was as follows:

> The National Council of Camp Fire Girls believes that spiritual development is essential to a healthy, wholesome personality and recognizes the importance of the church and synagogue and of religious experience and teachings in the life of a girl. The spiritual values of the church and synagogue are basic to the Camp Fire Girls program and the Camp Fire Girls Law. Each part of this Law is related to ethical living, encouraging an appreciation for God's world, emphasizing the dignity of individual human worth and character, and recognizing that service to others is one of the essentials of full living, all of which contributes to the spiritual atmosphere or climate that pervades the whole of life.[57]

Wohelo campers, counselors, and colleagues revered Charlotte as a wise and loving mother figure who possessed mystical qualities. For her girl campers, she championed creativity, beauty, friendship, physical fitness, sewing and dressmaking, crafts (jewelry, pottery, weaving), cooking, hiking, boating, fire making, cleanliness, child rearing, camping, management, personal achievement, group achievement, and horsemanship. She saw a beautiful world in which the feminine ideal, as she came to know and define it, was slipping away. Charlotte described her deeply held beliefs and attitudes about growing up female in American society in an interview published in the *New York Times* on March 17, 1912. Therein, she lamented:

> Many modern girls do not learn how to cook at all; boarding house and hotel life make it seem unnecessary; they do not learn how to sew; dressmakers, and, more especially, ready-to-wear clothing supply their needs. Thus they are robbed of two great pleasures which the centuries have fitted them to love—cooking and dressmaking; and of the development which they might gain from the pleasant tasks. Biscuits? The bakery provides them. Gowns? It costs less to buy them at the stores than it would cost to make them in the home and, on the whole, they are better

made by the wholesale manufacturers than they were at home in the old days.

Women's lives have almost wholly lost the joy of real creative work; and, at the same time, much discipline, the discipline of necessary tasks, no longer is to be found in them. With what great pleasure I for the first time made one of my own dresses when I was 13 years old! No game I ever played gave me one-half as much delight.[41]

Charlotte's intangible qualities and personal magnetism appear in the letters of Emily, who knows Charlotte only by her Indian name, Hiiteni. One of Charlotte's most devoted admirers was assistant camp director, Marguerite (Peggy) Smith, about whom Halsey Gulick wrote in *The Wohelo Bird* in 1928: "She [Peggy Smith] loves and lives Wohelo just as much as I, but the difference is that she is able to do and does a great deal more active work with you [the campers and counselors]."

Peggy Smith, counselors, and campers honored Hiiteni by writing and sharing poetry and songs about her. Peggy Smith wrote the following poem titled "Hiiteni" in 1928:

The dewdrops on the flower before the rising sun,
The colors in the eastern sky before the day's begun,
The cold gray mist of early dawn enshrouding the lake and mountain
Are mysteries of life revealing Thee in the fountain.

The rocks softened by moss and glistening with mica,
Night's brightest candles, Altair, Arcturus, and Vega,
The pine trees dripping with rain drops or glistening in the sun
Are messages from Thee of life's seriousness and fun.

The sparkle of the dewdrop or the color in the sky,
The cold gray mist—the gray rocks, night's brightest candles and the
    pine tree sigh,
The love of Hiiteni—her soul, her ideals true,
Her twinkling of fun and all the joys that must accrue.

O Hiiteni, Hiiteni, more abundant life
God gave your spirit to us and now the time is rife
To open up our hearts to Him, for this most precious gift
Will guide us, cheer us, and protect and never let us drift.

Hiiteni herself listed her loves, as follows:

- I love Lake Sebago
- I love the pine-needled paths of the woods
- I love the plunge into the cold, clean lake and the glow over and through my body which comes after the plunge
- I love the color about me, gold, crimson, red, and all the shades of brown
- I love the feel of the wet clay as I mold it into form
- I love to shut my eyes and mold it, pressing it into shape
- I love to burn the old dead limbs of trees
- I love the smell of the burning leaves
- I love the mist-covered water
- I love the white-throat as he flits about me
- I love the sunset
- I love the distant mountains
- I love the Northern lights
- I love the clear, shining stars
- I love the moonlight on Lake Sebago
- I love to hear the loon's call
- I love the wind, its soft whisperings through the pines and aspens, and its thunderous dashing of waves against our rocks
- I love our bungalow where we eat and see the lake
- I love the craft house and cliff houses and each tent
- I love Precious, our pony, and Snow-flake, our white horse
- More than all, I love the girl who comes here summers.[58]

In August 1918, Luther and Charlotte toured US military camps in Europe on behalf of the YMCA. Upon their return the *New York Times* published Luther's impressions in an article titled, "Warns Women of Change; Will Meet Different Men When War Is Over, Says Dr. Gulick." The article was published March 31, 1918 and read:

> Dr. Luther H. Gulick, head of the organization known as the Camp Fire Girls, who has just returned after a visit of several months to the American army camps in France, issued the following statement yesterday with reference to conditions in France:
>
> Everywhere in America ... mothers and sisters and sweethearts are anxious as to the conditions which surround their men. We

have been given every facility for finding out the facts, both by the War Work Council of the Y. M. C. A. and by the American military authorities. The conditions in our own army in France have been so improved and cared for by General Pershing that there is a better opportunity for clean bodies and clean characters there than in our average American communities. Only one man out of 300 over there is incapacitated with those diseases which in the past have been supposed to be associated with army life. This is a much lower record than that which is here in America, in our own families, in our own men.

These men will not be the same boys who went over. They will be trained in outdoor life [i.e., living in camps, or camping]. They will be accustomed to recreation on a very much broader scale than that which the average American man has had. They will be men who are not familiar with having their social life connected primarily with anything that is lowering. Thus, the greatest thing that American women and girls can do is to prepare to live up to the level of the army that is coming back; to make home the most beautiful and interesting place there is; to know the arts of camping, outdoor cooking; to know how to make life happy and beautiful is the main thing.

These men will not come back caring to see you [girls and women] in khaki or doing military tactics. They will have had all and more of that than they care for, but to see you and be with you as women, women who are playing their own part rather than trying to play the man's part in the world. Be ready to welcome the finest, cleanest, strongest group of men that have ever been in an army in the world.

When our men come home they will be heroes, men who have gone through the fire and who have looked death straight in the eye and come back unafraid, men who have been purified by that experience. Let us all live up to this splendid possibility and preserve the fine things which have been created under the army conditions.

Five months later, on August 13, 1918, Luther Gulick, Jr. was dead. Charlotte found him unconscious about 5:30 in the morning at Wohelo, and he never recovered consciousness. Dorgan described what happened next:

A bright day dawned, a memorable one in the lives of the campers. It was water carnival day, and Dr. Gulick lay dead in his house on top of the cliffs at the water's edge. The sports were held; death was not allowed to interfere. Charlotte Gulick saw to that, understanding that it was the way Luther Gulick would want it.

In her gracious way Mrs. Gulick greeted the neighbors who came for the water sports, talked to them in everyday fashion. When one asked for the Doctor he was told that the Doctor was dead.

Later Dr. Gulick's body was taken to Springfield and interred in the cemetery there, but before that a simple ceremony was held at camp. The casket was flag-draped and banked with wild ferns and flowers—no artificiality was present. The Negro helpers were present at the ceremony. The Gulick family joined in the singing. No tears were shed, Mrs. Gulick and the children knowing that they were following the Doctor's wish. However, behind the scenes there were tears, for who is so brave as always to keep them back?"[56]

Hiiteni ordered the water carnival (Water Sports Day) to go forward despite the death of Timanous. "The girls went through that day in a mood of solemn tribute to their beloved Timanous. At sunset the last 'war' canoes swept down the lake past Hiiteni standing erect on the bluff above them, as dozens of paddles flashed high in final salute."

A camper named Olivia P. Fentress captured the feeling of that day in a letter to her parents dated August 13, 1918:

Mother & Daddy dearest,
This morning at dawn dear Timanous quietly & comfortably passed away. You know how he has always had heart trouble & the strain of tending to the practice for Water Sports Day and the intense war work (the gov. reports) has been too much for him. He has not been at all strong this summer & lately I've noticed it more than ever. At our daily morning services he has had a sad far far away expression in his eyes & face. It brought the tears to my eyes to look at him. The family is so very brave. Today is Water Sports Day and Hiiteni's first wish was that things should be carried on just as Timanous would have wished to have them to do. I am sure camp will continue the same as usual for the rest of the time.[59]

On September 27, 1918, Charlotte wrote a long letter to all members of the Camp Fire Girls' organization throughout the United States. An excerpt of the letter follows:

> It is because [Timanous'] desires were unselfish that we cannot mourn, but rejoice, believing that he is still here and in greater measure guiding and loving us. It is too wonderful. As I sit here writing this letter in this little wooden shack, which was built for him and called Wakanahit, meaning "house of inspiration," my heart goes out to each one of you and I long to have his "guiding spirit" become to you what it is to me during these days which the world calls dark. We gave him the name Timanous, meaning "guiding spirit," here on these rocks, little realizing what it would mean, now that we cannot see him but must feel him.[57]

On July 28, 1928, ten years after Luther's death, Hiiteni died after a long illness. Emily was present at Camp Wohelo the summer of Hiiteni's death. Emily met Hiiteni before her death and at least twice visited Hiiteni's empty "shack" after her death. Emily wrote about these experiences in her letters. The way in which camp leaders reacted to Hiiteni's death, as per her instructions, likely helped Emily deal with the deaths of her younger brother Bud (1944), her father Abraham (1957), her mother Estelle (1970), and her own son Morgan (1972).

Halsey (John Halsey Gulick), the youngest Gulick offspring, was born on December 27, 1899. He had taken the reins of the Luther Gulick Camps in the summer of 1928 as his mother grew weaker from illness. Halsey received his formal education at the Ethical Culture School (founded by Felix Adler in 1878) in New York, Phillips Exeter Academy in Massachusetts, and Princeton University in New Jersey (class of 1923). He was the swimming coach at Lehigh University in Bethlehem, Pennsylvania, between 1923 and 1927 whence he resigned to join Dr. Joseph E. Raycroft (1867–1955) at Princeton University for a year.[60-61] Dr. Raycroft was chairman of health and physical education at Princeton University, 1911–1936.[62]

When Halsey became director of Wohelo in 1928, he said the experience was "a revelation." He continued, "Although I was brought up in the atmosphere of Wohelo, I have been away for the past five years and I had no idea how much I had missed until my return." In addition to directing the Luther Gulick Camps each summer, Halsey taught physical education at two private schools during the school year and eventually became headmaster of Proctor Academy in Andover, New Hampshire in 1936, a position he held for seventeen years. He retired from Proctor Academy in 1953 at age fifty-three (his father died at age fifty-two) to devote his energies full time to the Luther Gulick Camps.[63] Emily, like many of the Wohelo campers, thought Halsey was adorable.

Map of Sebago Lake in Maine, United States of America. Note that north is on the right side and west is on the top of the illustration, and that Sebago Lake is white and Raymond Cape is black in the illustration. Lake Sebago Railroad Station is on the left hand side of map, at the south tip of lake and Wohelo is at the site designated "Camp Site. Image credit: Wohelo Camp Archives, Raymond, Maine.

Heavenlies Rock granite outcropping, Wohelo Camp, Sebago Lake, Maine (postcard). Image credit: Sophian Archives, Fairway, Kansas.

Charlotte Vetter Gulick (Hiiteni) in a canoe, Sebago Lake, Maine, circa 1915–1925. Image credit: Wohelo Camp Archives, Raymond, Maine.

Dr. Luther Halsey Gulick, Jr. and family, circa 1910–1915, Wohelo Camp, Raymond, Maine. Image was probably taken by Mrs. Charlotte Gulick. Image credit: Wohelo Camp Archives, Raymond, Maine.

Halsey Gulick, Wohelo camp director, 1928, with "Jill." Image credit: Wohelo Camp Archives, Raymond, Maine.

CHAPTER THREE:

Wohelo: Organization and Campers

The forests of Wohelo are populated with pine, balsam, spruce, maple, oak, beech, poplar, and hemlock trees, according to Wohelo publication materials in 1928. Reindeer moss, which Hiiteni especially loved, once covered many rocks. In 1928 five islands in the lake belonged to the Luther Gulick Camps. The Gulicks cleared a fifteen-acre tract of land to conduct a small farming establishment and build a horse stable and two riding circles. There were tennis, but no basketball, courts.

The Luther Gulick Camps in 1928 owned more than fifty boats and canoes, including six thirty-four-foot war canoes, five sailing canoes, a Barnegat sailboat and two motor boats. The canoes were made by Old Town Canoe Company (founded around 1900) of Old Town, Maine. A diving tower and springboard dared at the edge of the lake.

The fifty-three buildings on the Wohelo property (at the time Emily attended) included a dining room and kitchen, a building for the library, charts and exhibits, a building for crafts, an office, hostess and director bungalows, two cliff houses, a bungalow for sleeping quarters, and twenty-two tents pitched on wooden platforms. Emily and three other girls slept on cots in their tent atop Heavenlies Rock. The three girls were:

- Susan (Sue) Miller of Winnetka, Illinois and Smith College in Northampton, Massachusetts;
- Margaret (Peggy) Wade of Syracuse, New York and National Cathedral School, Washington, DC; and

- Margaret (Mac) Frothingham of New Canaan, Connecticut.

Halsey Gulick and Peggy Smith oversaw five units of girl campers at Wohelo in 1928. Each unit contained around fifteen girls. The names of the five units were Heavenlies, Barracks, Haeremai, Boulders, and Lewa. A head counselor ("H.C." in Emily's letters) led each unit. The head counselors in 1928 were:

- Heavenlies: Frances (Frannie) Cooper of Syracuse, New York
- Barracks: Helen (Dub) Davis of North Conway, New Hampshire
- Haeremai: Barbara (Bobby) Fort of East Orange, New Jersey
- Boulders: Margaret (Marty) Hedden of East Orange, New Jersey
- Lewa: Molly Radford of Chicago, Illinois.

Halsey declared in the 1928 issue of *The Wohelo Bird* that each head counselor looked "after her own unit as if it were a separate camp belonging to her, which she had built up, yet never los[t] sight of the fact that she was working together with four other units for Wohelo as a whole."

"Junior" counselors were Ruth (Rastus) Chapman of New Haven, Connecticut and Northampton, Massachusetts; Helen (Teddy) Feeney of Brooklyn, New York; Mrs. Charles G. Hall (Mooney) of Boston, Massachusetts; Elizabeth (Bob) McCurdy of Ann Arbor, Michigan; Mary Lois (Lois) Paschal of Chevy Chase, Maryland; Ruth Price of Monrovia, California; Eleanor (Spotty) Schreyer of Milton, Pennsylvania; Elizabeth (Betty) Selkirk of Albany, New York; Jane Shurmer of Cleveland, Ohio; and Eleanor (Tenny) Ten Eyck of Westfield, New Jersey.

"Trusted Girl" counselors were returning campers given added responsibility by Hiiteni. Sue Miller was the Trusted Girl counselor to Emily, Mac, and Peg in Emily's tent group in 1928. In 1921, Charlotte wrote a letter to Trusted Girl counselor Dottie Merrill, as follows:

> Dear Dotty:
> You will soon be entering into your new camp life. There will be many things to which you must adjust yourself and in the excitement of the first busy days I shall not have a chance to talk with you personally. So before you come I am taking this quiet opportunity to tell you some of the things that will help you have a successful summer.
> You are going to be a lieutenant to the captain of your team,

your head counselor. You will have three girls in your tent who will be depending on you for direct guidance in all they do. There are fifteen girls, two "trusted girl" counselors, two of you counselors [sic] and your head counselor, in your group. Your unit must be organized carefully so that each girl feels her definite part in the whole. This requires a great deal of loving thought.

A beautiful older-sister relationship is possible between you and all the camp girls, and especially the three in your tent. Girls of this age are sensitive and responsive and your influence with them can be a sacred responsibility. Many of them have never been away from home before. You must make it your business that none of them are homesick or unhappy. Make them feel your interest in them from the very start.

One of the things that seem to go with the joys of camp is mosquitoes. They last only a short time and are not annoying if proper precaution is taken against them. See that the mosquito nettings are tucked around your girls before you get into bed. Be a good sport about it, and your girls will reflect your attitude.

As soon as the morning bugle blows a counselor hops out of bed and hustles her girls down to the deck for a dip. Prompt attendance at breakfast, pride in the perfect neatness in the tent, depend on the feeling you inspire in your girls. When craft hour comes you must know where each is working and see that she is not neglecting any of the opportunities offered to her. She will look to you for enthusiasm and advice in her work.

It has been our tradition to uphold the highest ideals in regard to the care of the body. Perhaps one of the most difficult things to meet is the candy problem, which has sometimes become quite serious because of the counselors' attitude towards it. We provide sufficient sweets. I ask your hearty co-operation in helping the girls to see the reasonableness of controlling their desire.

In order that camp may start on the very first day the girls come, it will be necessary for you to see that they unpack their trunks and arrange their clothes with care as quickly as possible. City clothes are hung in the various trunk houses.

Your head counselor is prepared to help you with any problem that may arise. And you must feel that I am eager to help you, too. Every day in the summer has its own part in the happy results. Don't let a single opportunity slip by.

The girls who will be under your care are going to be the leading women of the future. Yours is a thrilling opportunity with them. The camp influence will extend throughout the entire life of the girls. Will you help me make it the most glorious influence possible?

Affectionately yours,
Hiiteni[1]

In 1928 there were Second Year Trusted Girl counselors and First Year Trusted Girl counselors. The "Second Year Trusted Girl" counselors were:

- Fanniebelle (Junior) Allen of Meadville, Pennsylvania and the Knox School in Cooperstown, New York;
- Elizabeth (Betty) Bingham of West Newton, Massachusetts and Mount Vernon Seminary in Washington, DC;
- Catherine (Cay) Bolster of West Newton, Massachusetts and Burnham School in Northampton, Massachusetts;
- Susan (Sue) Miller of Winnetka, Illinois and Smith College, Northampton, Massachusetts (she was a member of Emily's tent group); and
- Virginia Smiley (Smiley) of Great Barrington, Massachusetts.

Sue Miller was likely the first Smith College student Emily had ever met. Emily later would attend Smith College.

The "First Year Trusted Girl" counselors were:

- Susan (Sue) Brockett of New Haven Connecticut and Wellesley College, Wellesley, Massachusetts;
- Julia (Julie) Denison of Cape Cottage, Maine;
- Louisa Ford of Elizabeth, Maine;
- Virginia Macomber of Providence, Rhode Island; and
- Anna Nichols of Kansas City, Missouri.

The camp employed individuals competent in many fields, including water sports (Jane Shurmer of Cleveland, Ohio and Robert Hertzler of Lancaster, Pennsylvania); horseback riding (Sherman [Shy] K. Crockett of Cambridge, Massachusetts; John Culbertson of Lansdowne, Pennsylvania; Raymond Eastup of South Windham, Maine; and Dana McConkey of South Casco, Maine); jewelry (Floyd N. Ackley of New York City and Eleanor Schreyer of Milton, Pennsylvania); weaving (Katherine Alden of Boston, Massachusetts); pottery (Elizabeth Selkirk of Albany, New York); nature lore (Ruth Price of Monrovia, California and Ruth Chapman of Northampton, Massachusetts);

music (Mrs. Charles G. Hall of Boston, Massachusetts) and Helen Feeney of Brooklyn, New York); farming and gardening (Wendell Brown, also known as "Farmer Brown," of Greenwich, Connecticut); and tennis (Mary Lois Paschal of Chevy Chase, Maryland). The camp nurse in 1928 was May Fern MacLeod (Mac) of Portland, Maine. The bugler, known as "Taps," was Robert Bonner of Portland, Maine.

The beloved cooks at Wohelo were Mr. and Mrs. W. G. Tillman (Wayne and Emily) of Princeton, New Jersey. The dining room girls were Helen Cowles of Portland, Maine; Carolyn Hatch of Portland, Maine; and Evelyn Cummings of South Casco, Maine. Sam Cummings and Charles Watkins, both of South Casco, Maine, oversaw building and grounds and general utility, respectively.

The following seventy-four girls attended Wohelo in 1928, according to Wohelo materials issued to each camper:

- Suzanne Arguimbau, Glenbrook, Connecticut
- Lois Ashley, Binghamton, New York
- Jean Baldwin, Upper Montclair, New Jersey and Choate School, Brookline, Massachusetts
- Barbara (Bobbie) Baker, Madison, New Jersey
- Muriel (Mu) Behrens, New York City
- Frances Bell, Hubbard Woods, Illinois
- Doris (Dorrie) Benson, West Newton, Massachusetts
- Eleanor (Bing) Bingham, West Newton, Massachusetts
- Bettina (Tink) Blanding, Syracuse, New York and Hartridge School, Plainfield, New Jersey
- Elizabeth (Brooksie) Brooks, Syracuse, New York
- Mary Adeline Cline, Cleveland, Ohio and Knox School, Cooperstown, New York
- Elizabeth (Betty) Cluff, Plandome, New York
- Nancy Cluff, Plandome, New York
- Barbara (Weenie) Colbron, New Canaan, Connecticut
- Virginia (Ginger) Condict, Madison, New Jersey
- Sally Drew, Newtonville, Massachusetts
- Cynthia (Cynnie) Dudley, Syracuse, New York
- Mary E. (Billie) Dudley, St. Augustine, Florida and Birmingham School, Birmingham, Pennsylvania
- Deborah Ann (Debby) Durstine, Scarsdale, New York and Masters School, Dobbs Ferry, New York

- Ellen (Babs) Eastman, Newton Centre, Massachusetts
- Barbara (Barbie) Eaton, West Newton, Massachusetts
- Marjorie (Midge) Estabrook, Newton, Massachusetts and Smith College, Northampton, Massachusetts
- Betty (Frenchy) French, Springfield, Vermont and Emma Willard School, Troy, New York
- Janet (Frenchy) French, Springfield, Vermont and Emma Willard School, Troy, New York
- Margaret (Mack) Frothingham, New Canaan, Connecticut
- Jane Gehring, Portland, Maine
- Adelaide Greene, Boston, Massachusetts
- Caroline (Boots) Hales, Oak Park, Illinois
- Hildegarde Hathaway, Brighton, Massachusetts
- Harriet (Happy) Hilts, Albany, New York
- Mary (Red) Holmes, Fayetteville, New York
- Eunice (Jimmie) Jameson, Chevy Chase, Maryland
- Elizabeth (Betty) Knowland, Syracuse, New York
- Frances [Fritz] Laundon, Cleveland, Ohio
- Barbara (Bobby) Lewis, Syracuse, New York
- Edith (Kink) Longsdorf, Newton Centre, Massachusetts
- Leonora McClure, Tarrytown, New York
- Susan (Sue) Merritt, Madison, New York
- Elizabeth (Betsy) Nevitt, Oshkosh, Wisconsin
- Dorothy (Dottie) Newton, West Newton, Massachusetts
- Katherine (Kittie) Ober, St. Paul, Minnesota
- Jean Palmer, Madison, New Jersey
- Frances (Frankie) Phillips, Providence, Rhode Island
- Margaret Price, Monrovia, California
- Frieda (Freddie) Purdum, Queens Village, Long Island, New York
- Eleanor (Roger) Rogers, Quincy, Illinois and Emma Willard School, Troy, New York
- Helen Rogers, Quincy, Illinois
- Mary (Rupe) Rupert, Pompano, Florida
- Janice (Jannie) Smith, Syracuse, New York and Miss Porter's School, Farmington, Connecticut
- Marguerite (Muggins) Smith, Syracuse, New York
- Nancy Smith, Pittsfield, Massachusetts
- Emily Sophian, Kansas City, Missouri
- Flora Agnes (Flea) Sporborg, Syracuse, New York
- Helen Ruth Starrett, Madison, New Jersey
- Barbara (Bobbie) Stearns, New Canaan, Connecticut

- Mary Millis (Mitch) Storr, Passaic, New Jersey
- Betty Joy Street, Richmond, Virginia
- Edna (Teddy) Ten Eyck, Westfield, New Jersey
- Marion (Tommy) Thompson, Syracuse, New York
- Mary Jane (Judy) Thompson, Syracuse, New York
- Margaret (Tim) Tomlinson, Milton, Pennsylvania
- Nancy Townsend, New York City
- Dorothea (Babs) Van Duyn, Syracuse, New York
- Eleanor (Ellie) Vincent, Syracuse, New York
- Margaret (Peggy) Wade, Syracuse, New York and National Cathedral School, Washington, DC
- Jean Ward, Winnetka, Illinois
- Lois (Lovey) Warren Cumberland Mills, Maine and Miss Wheeler's School, Providence, Rhode Island
- Marion (Westie) West, New Rochelle, New York
- Dorothy (Dottie) Wilson, Syracuse New York and Masters School, Dobbs Ferry, New York
- Elaine (Lee) Wood, Uphams Cor., Massachusetts
- Mary Frances (Woody) Wood, Decatur, Illinois
- Emily Jane (E.J.) Wood, Decatur, Illinois
- Jane Wonders, St. Louis, Missouri

Charlotte Gulick required purchase by campers of the following items, which were listed in a booklet:

- Two pairs of dark bloomers
- Three white middy blouses (unbleached blouses without color trimming)
- Four French peasant blue blouses
- Heavy dark blue coat sweater
- Scarlet bathing suit
- Bathing cap
- Black middy tie, scarlet middy tie
- Six pairs black stockings
- Two pairs tennis shoes
- One pair water-tight shoes
- Official riding habit
- Raincoat
- Worsted jersey (navy blue)
- White belt for bathing suit
- Marine middy hat

- Appropriate undergarments and pajamas can be secured from our outfitters
- Besides these items of wearing apparel, the girl needs only her traveling suit
- One pair of woolen blankets and one army blanket
- One very large rubber blanket (60 inches by 90 inches)
- Three pillow cases, one pillow
- Three ordinary or flannelette sheets
- Four bath towels
- Two laundry bags
- Jackknife
- Flashlight
- Steamer trunks or large dress suit cases *only* are allowed in camp
- *Trunks as well as all garments* MUST HAVE *the owner's name*
- In order to have uniform color and design, all necessary outfit should be secured from our official outfitters. Camp Supplies, Inc., 52 Chauncy Street, Boston, Mass. Send to them for order and measurement blank. Early orders receive better service.

Jane Wonders, who attended Wohelo in 1928 with Emily, described the bathing suits, bloomers, middie blouses, and ties in a letter dated November 4, 1993:

> Please note the bathing suits in [19]27 and [19]28. Two layers of tightly knit thick [scarlet] wool. The under one had legs about 3" or 4" long. It was worn alone only for morning dip. Otherwise we also had the oversuit with skirt but no legs. The whole was held together with a white belt. Underneath some also wore a bra. ... That was also the time of pleated wool serge bloomers and long black stockings, even on hot days. The blue middie blouse was for weekdays with a black silk tie—white with red tie for Sundays—and no breach of uniform, ever.[3]

Heavenlies tent, Wohelo Camp, Maine, circa 1928–1929. Image credit: Wohelo Camp Archives, Raymond, Maine.

Sivad cottage, Wohelo Camp, Maine. Image credit: Wohelo Camp Archives, Raymond, Maine.

Wohelo camper and staff group image in four sections, 1928.
Emily Sophian wrote the names of campers and staff directly on
the image. Image credit: Sophian Archives, Fairway, Kansas.

CHAPTER FOUR:

Emily Sophian's Wohelo Letters

On the evening of June 26, 1928, Estelle and Abraham waved goodbye to Emily and Bud inside the cavernous Beaux Arts-style Union Station, constructed in Kansas City in 1914. Anna and Mit Nichols, also bound for Wohelo and Timanous, respectively, joined Emily and Bud on the Chicago, Burlington, and Quincy Railroad train. Camp counselor Molly Radford joined Emily and Anna on the train trip between Chicago and Sebago Lake Railroad Station.

Emily Sophian wrote to her parents almost every day—at least once each day and sometimes twice—beginning only hours after departing from the Union Station in Kansas City, Missouri. Her first letter, addressed to "Dr. and Mrs. A. Sophian, Georgian Court, Kansas City, Mo.," read:

> Tuesday
> Dear Mother and Dad:
> Well, after weeping thoroughly, and long, at eleven o'clock [P.M.] your homesick daughter (decidedly cheered up by reading and finishing the book Aunt Gertie gave her) is going to attempt to write you a letter and unburden her mind.
> Anna's lower is just opposite mine, so I gave her my ticket and stuff to take care of. You see, I was kind of scared of the conductor – was afraid I wouldn't know how to act if he asked me for it, or wanted to punch a hole in it or something. (Rather vague all that, isn't it) – TIME OUT – We just hit another skunk! That's

the second one in less than five minutes and does this train smell
– Whoopee! S'terrible.

Say, please tell Aunt Gertie for me that the book was nifty
– Awfully cute! I'll send it back to-morrow maybe, and will get
another one in Chicago. I think mother will like it, but it's not
exciting enough to interest dad, I don't think.

Well, this train is lurching "woise and woise" and pretty soon
you won't be able to read this scrawl any more (if you've been able
to this far) –

Best love Emmy

P.S. Please write soon (right away)

On June 27, Emily wrote the following letter on Morrison Hotel (located
at Clark and Madison Streets, Chicago, Illinois)[1] stationary while staying
overnight in Chicago:

Wednesday
Dear Mother and Dad:

We got into Chicago around eight thirty this morning after
a h---luva nite. Gee, was I ever homesick! I feel much better now
that I've seen Bud, but I still retain a sort of sinking feeling –
Nosso good.

Frankie and Bud Clark met us and brought us to this hotel.
Bud and Mit [Nichols] were here, but they were both dead to the
world. It was just as good that they were though, because Anna
lost Mit's bag with all his stuff. Bud C. and Frank went back to the
station to look for it, and things were going swell when Mit woke
up. Then there was "heaven" to pay – Gee, was he mad! Anyhow,
the boys found the bag, and peace reigned until Bud S. woke up.
Then the noise began again – And how!

Bud C., Frankie, Anna, and I had lunch at Marshall Fields
[department store]. I don't know where Bud S. and Mit ate, but
they met us at the Garrick Theater later, where we saw "Excess
Baggage." It was a good play and we all enjoyed it.

Anna and I had dinner at Terrace Garden, with some of Mr.
Nichols' friends. There were two other girls there too. We danced
some, but it wasn't much fun because the men were too old. Mr.
Nichols was awfully nice tho.

We got on the train at nine o'clock. It's twenty of twelve now,
and I've met some awfully cute girls – (I can't think of their names
but they're cute anyhow) – I've also read a Detective Magazine

your son bought – By the way – the first thing that guy did when he saw me was borrow two dollars.

Say hello to my relatives for me please – Also to Aunt Gertie and Uncle B. L.

Please write soon. I miss you both atrociously –

All my love –

Emmy

P.S. This is the bumpiest train I've ever ridden on, and it doesn't make writing easy, so please excuse blots and scribbling –

On June 28, Emily wrote:

Thursday

Dear Mother and Dad:

We've been on this terribly sticky and hot train all day, but aside from the fact that the food is rotten and <u>awfully</u> expensive, everything is fine. I met an awfully cute girl – Frances Laundon [also on her way to Camp Wohelo] – from Cleveland, Ohio, and I like her a lot. We're sleeping to-gether to-nite.

Our train just pulled into Boston. It's ten o'clock P.M., and both Frances and I wanted to get out and walk around. Unfortunately, Molly [Radford], our councilor [there were various spellings of this word in 1928, including councilor, counsellor and counselor; Emily used "councilor"] who is darling, wouldn't let us, so at present we are both curled up in our berth writing letters. We're profiting by the lapse of jerks and shakes of the train to do that. We're going to read after that, and then probably talk. Our train gets into Portland around five A.M. so I don't think we'll get much sleep – do you?

Bud is on this train and is already the center of a bunch of noisy kids his age – He's really awfully cute but he is acting more or less like a gentleman so you needn't worry.

I miss you both terribly. I'm much more homesick at nite than I am during the day anyhow, and besides, I feel rather shaky at the prospect of camp to-morrow –

Please write me soon, but I left you the wrong address – You should write me c/o Luther-Gulick Camps, South Casco, Maine. Don't forget –

Loads of love

Emmy –

P.S. Anna lost all her money so I've lent her $4.00 already – My kid brother borrowed $2.00, and the rest is flying – I haven't got more than $15.00 if that much – Dad's $5.00 will sure come in handy – More love

The Maine Central Railroad (White Mountain Division, built in 1870) linked Union Station, Portland, with Sebago Lake Railroad Station at the foot of Sebago Lake. Wohelo campers who arrived by railroad climbed off the train at the Sebago Lake Railroad Station and boarded a steamer that took them north across Sebago Lake to the landing at the camp. The water distance between the Sebago Lake Railroad Station and Wohelo dock was about eight miles.

Soon after reaching Wohelo and her tent on June 28, 1928, Emily wrote the following letter to her parents:

Thursday
Dear Mother and Dad:
We got to camp this morning at an ungodly hour, and tho the weather was freezing, I love it. I was awfully homesick for a while, and felt all lost and lonesome, but I'm getting over it, and I'm sure I'll have an awfully nice time – At least I hope I will –
There wasn't much doing to-day. We had breakfast as soon as we got here. Then we were assigned our units. I'm in "Heavenly." Our head councilor is Frannie Cooper, from Syracuse. The Junior Councilor in my tent is Sue Miller, an awfully cute girl. The other girls are Peggy Wade, and Mac Frothingham, who is also new.
There was swimming at eleven. I didn't go in – I got cold feet.
We slept all afternoon. After dinner we went to the craft house where they sang songs. Halsey also introduced the Councilors. It was fun and I like it. It's time to go to bed now, and I feel darn near tears, so more tomorrow –
Love
Emmy –

On June 29, Estelle wrote the following letter to Emily:

Friday
Emmy dear:
We forgot to put your bathrobe in the trunk. I sent it to you parcels [*sic*] post to-day – knowing you will need it –

Only this morning we received the letter you wrote on the train Tuesday evening – You should not have read all night You know that is not good for your eyes – Be sure to write Aunt Gertie to thank her for the book –

You know that the railroad ticket you had included your return trip. Be sure to take care of it or have someone do so –

Be sure to write me in detail your impression of the camp – the girls – the director and councillors. In that way I will have a picture of your environment in my mind's eye – and will try to see you moving about in your new locale.

Needless to tell you that it is deathly quiet here without you and Bud –

Had luncheon with Mrs. Bush yesterday. She is very enthusiastic about their trip to Wildwood and is speaking of buying a place of her own –

Much love
Mother

Emily's letter of June 30, read:

Saturday
Dear Mother and Dad:

Bugle blew at seven this morning, and, summoning all my courage, I went in for morning dip. You may have thought Walloon [Lake] cold, but take it from me, Sebago [Lake] is the iciest lake in the U.S.A. It's terrible, but I felt [word?] when I got out.

After breakfast we made our cots and cleaned up the tent. Then I proceeded to write you. Listen, I haven't missed a day, but I haven't heard from either of you <u>once</u>. I think you are both <u>awful</u>, and I don't mean perhaps. Say Mother, I thought that you packed my bath robe in my duffle bag, so I didn't look for it to put it in the trunk. Therefore, I haven't got it, so will you please send it to me – I need it.

Around ten o'clock, bugle blew for Sivad. It's a sort of morning services which is awfully impressive and nice. Halsey reads something suitable or other – (I couldn't make much out of it, but I know it was suitable) – Then we sang hymns, and camp songs and we learnt a council fire song. [Council Fire was held every Monday night. Emily did not capitalize the term "Council Fire" in her letters] Sivad is <u>quite</u> the thing – I like it a lot.

This afternoon after rest hour we hiked into South Casco for ice cream. It was the longest three miles I ever walked, and if it hadn't been for the thought of the ice cream I would eventually get, I doubt if I should ever had reached the blooming place – (which can't compare with Boyne [Michigan]). I saw the kid brother there – he looks grand, and refused to give me any of his ice cream. I didn't care tho, because I consumed a quart of my own anyhow – Walking back was terrible. This evening was the [word?] – We got odds and ends, and rags in the attick [*sic*], and went in costumes. You should have seen some of them – Whee! I went as a Missouri Scarecrow, and I sure looked the part. I had a grand time, and am just dead. Wow I have to turn in and wrestle with the mosquitoes.

Please write.

Love Emmy

P.S. Hasn't Skinny written me yet? If so, why not?

P.S. Please tell Aunt Gertie that all the girls are crazy about "Hip Elizabeth." There are four or five of them reading it now

Sivad was a group get-together held in a cottage on Sivad Point on Sebago. Hewson explained that "Sivad" is not an Indian word, but simply the word "Davis" spelled backwards. The Davis family owned the property before the Gulicks purchased it.[2]

South Casco is located on the northeast edge of Sebago Lake, at the origin of Raymond Neck. South Casco separated from the town of Raymond (Raymondtown) in 1841. Raymond was named after Captain William Raymond (1758–1834) to whom the General Court of Massachusetts (Maine was then part of Massachusetts) granted the township in 1767 in consideration of his services in the (unsuccessful) siege of Quebec in 1690. However, Captain Raymond, who lived in Beverly, Massachusetts, never settled in Raymond. Instead, Captain Joseph Dingley settled Raymond in 1771, and the town was incorporated in 1803, taking its name from Captain Raymond.[3]

American novelist Nathaniel Hawthorne (1804–1864), born in Salem, Massachusetts, revered Sebago Lake, calling it his "Garden of Eden." During the period 1816–1819, he lived in Raymond with his widowed mother (his father, Captain Hawthorne had died at sea) and his two sisters.[4] His mother's brother, Richard Manning, had built a home for them in Raymond. Hawthorne later attended Bowdoin College in Brunswick, Maine, which was only about twenty-seven miles to the east of Raymond. Hawthorne wrote about Maine, as follows:

"I lived in Maine like a bird of the air, so perfect was the freedom I enjoyed. But it was there I first got my cursed habits of solitude. How well I recall the summer days, when, with my gun, I roamed at will through the woods of Maine. Everything is beautiful in youth, for all things are allowed to it then."[5]

Among Hawthorne's greatest works were *The Scarlet Letter*, *The House of the Seven Gables*, and *Twice-Told Tales*. Emily, who aspired to become an authoress, undoubtedly contemplated Hawthorne during her trips to South Casco.

Dr. Gulick was a strong public advocate of rest and wrote a book on the topic aptly titled *Exercise and Rest*.[6] In a *New York Times* article titled ""Says Work and Play Should Come in Turn; Dr. Gulick Favors Frequent Periods of Rest" and published on April 18, 1905, he "insisted on alternate periods of rest and activity in life. Continuous work fatigues the brain cells, said he, and periods of rest should be followed by periods of intense activity," such as Emily's walk to South Casco for ice cream after rest hour on her cot in the tent. In his book *Exercise and Rest* (1910), he wrote:

What is the relation between exercise and rest? Work is that at which we must continue, whether interesting or not, whether we are tired or not. It used to be thought that the prime requisite of rest was the use of faculties other than those involved in the labor of the day. But there is such a thing as fatigue which goes deeper than daily work. We can work so hard as to become exhausted—too exhausted for any kind of work. Perhaps this is *will* fatigue. It is coming to be regarded as fundamentally true that rest from such fatigue demands continuity; that, for example, four periods of fifteen minutes each of rest is not the equivalent of one hour's rest, that a man who goes on a vacation and takes half an hour of his business work every day, is doing the same thing as the man who had a horse with a sore back. He kept the saddle on only a few minutes each day, but the sore did not have a chance to heal. Rest periods must be sufficiently consecutive to overcome consecutive fatigue.[6]

Luther Gulick wrote in *Philosophy of Play*, referenced above, the following:

• Character is formed predominantly during leisure hours.

- Children should be included in all family conferences.
- Household tasks can be made delightful experiences.
- The dance is one of the best media for healthful relaxation.
- Everyone should play some musical instrument—tom-tom if nothing else.
- To make a person well, you must make him happy.
- Exercise without the play drive is useless.
- One cannot rest on a single achievement.
- Drudgery is obnoxious and is unnecessary.
- The pessimist is an unhealthy man.
- Education falls short if it equips us only for work.
- Many people are emotional sluggards; they need awakening activities.
- Our country has little use for youth who were soft, lazy, and have headaches (during World War I).
- Play is that which we do free from any economic lash or compulsion.
- It seems as curious to exercise for health as to eat for health.
- School property should be kept open to serve all people around the clock.
- Camps properly run are a laboratory for life.
- Ideals without a practical basis are idle dreams.[8]

On July 1, 1928, Emily wrote:

Sunday
Dear Mother and Dad:
    You're a fine pair you are, haven't written your only daughter once – Gee, you're terrible – I wish you'd at least drop me a card! S'not asking too much is it?
    To-day being Sunday, we got to sleep till a quarter of eight instead of a quarter of seven. Sivad was at eleven. It lasted longer than usual, but after that, there was nothing else to do. We spent the day reading, writing letters and fooling around. Will write more to-morrow when something happens –
    Bestest love
    Emmy
P.S. Halsey raced his speed boat at Portland to-day and won all three races even tho had turned over in one.

The Gulicks deliberately inserted non-structured periods into the campers' lives. In his paper titled "The Social Function of Play," Luther Gulick, Jr. wrote:

> Recreation is that to which one turns from the strenuous part of life and through which one seeks recuperation, rest and change. Play is that which one does when one is free to pursue the deepest things that one chooses to do, for the joy of the working, not from compulsion, not from economic necessity, nor the last of public opinion. Play is responsible for the splendid achievements of human life, for it is self-actuated.[55]

Emily's letter dated July 2, 1928, said:

> Monday
>
> Dear Mother and Dad:
>
> I got Mother's letter this noon, and it was so good to hear from one of you. I wish it would happen more often and I wish Dad could find time to drop me a line. How about it, "fawthah"? Please do.
>
> I didn't go in for dip this morning because it was too cold. I washed at the fountain instead – More convenient but not as much fun.
>
> After breakfast and Sivad, the war canoes were launched. It was one of the prettiest spectacles I have ever witnessed – Gee – it was great!
>
> After it was over our unit went over to the farm and rode. I had a h---uva horse. It's name was "Sticky" and I had a terrible time, and on top of that if I wanted it to go fast, it walked and lagged behind all the others, and if I wanted to walk, the blooming animal tried to show me how well it could race – Holy mackerel – What a ride!
>
> When I came back I passed my 135 yd. swimming test. Now I can go [on] all the dock[s] – gosh, I'm happy!
>
> This afternoon after rest hour, we had jewelry. It's more fun. I'll come back quite the accomplished creature – (Ha! Ha!)
>
> To-nite was council fire. It was glorious. We come in singing, and then we sit down in triangle formation. I can't tell you what it's like. It's something that has to be seen. More to-morrow. I have to go to bed and the mosquitoes now – Gee – those insects are terrible.

Write quick –
Best love
Emmy

Emily's July 3 letter read:

Tuesday
Dear Mother and Dad:
There was crew practice this morning for the first time. I went down and tried it – It's loads of fun, but oh – so different from regular paddling. Gee, I sure felt green. I was all warmed up tho when I went in for dip – (first time at dock) – and I had a terrible appetite at breakfast. You ought to see me eat – the food is <u>so</u> good.

After Sivad this morning, I went in swimming again and tried to pass my diving and breast-stroke test for water baby [Emily never capitalized "Water Baby"] – I didn't have much luck with either tho. Mother, I think you have me beat when it comes to breaststroke. You may make funny faces, but you get there. But with me, there doesn't seem to be any cooperation at all between my arms and legs – Such luck!

I forgot to say that I rowed around Wohelo Island – (also for water baby) – I had a terrible time. The oars aren't attached, and I felt (and was) so awkward – and you ought to see my blisters!

I hiked into South Casco this afternoon and got some ice cream. The weather was so hot that I got two cones – one double-dip chocolate, and one double-dip chocolate and vanilla. I wanted more but decided (of my own accord) against it.

Nothing much happened this evening – so more to-morrow. I'm having a gorgeous time, but I miss you something fierce, and I'm pretty homesick nights. Please write me – both of you.
Best love
Emmy –
P.S. Hasn't Skinny written me yet?

In 1928, the requirements for achieving status as a "Water Baby" at Camp Wohelo were:

Swimming
Swim 135 yards
Fall out of canoe and return to it

Breast stroke
Side stroke
Back stroke
Three plain front dives
Rowing
    Row islands
    Climb into boat from water
    Hiiteni push-off
    One good landing on each side
    Row well backward and forward, plain and with alternate oars
    Turn on a pivot
    Jump into boat from dock
    Final test
Paddling
    Paddle islands
    Paddle silently
    Make four good landings – two on each side, paddling on each side
    Change places in a canoe
    Final test
Knots
    Tie each of the following knots three times – square, slip, two half
    hitches
Shafer Method
    Oral quiz and one minute demonstration [The Shafer (Schafer, Schaefer)
    method was an early type of artificial respiration devised and named
    by Professor Schaefer of Edinburgh, Scotland, as carefully explained by
    Charlotte Gulick in her book *Emergencies* (pages 127–130). Charlotte
    wrote:

> Lay the person on his stomach on a level place. Turn the head
> to the left side, so that the mouth and nose are away from the
> ground. Either kneel by the side of the patient, or sit on his
> hips, and place both hands over the small of the back, with the
> thumbs nearly touching and spread out over the lowest ribs; then
> swing yourself forward, counting three slowly on this forward
> movement. Now quickly swing yourself backward, releasing
> the pressure, but keeping the hands on the body in the original
> position and the arms straight. In three more counts repeat this
> movement. This should be done ten or twelve times a minute
> without pausing between the movements. While one person is
> giving the artificial breathing others can be getting dry blankets

or hot-water bottles or they can be rubbing the arms or legs of the patient. There should be no attempt made to force the patient to drink anything until after breathing is restored.

Count [Water Baby song]

Water Baby was the first achievement level, followed by two higher levels of achievement—Water Witch and Water Queen. Water Witch requirements were:

Swimming
    Swim six strokes
    Make four dives
    Swim to Rookies [Island]
    Undress in deep water
    Rescue person fifty feet from dock—any carry but tired swimmer's
    Get cup in eight feet of water—surface dive in fair form
    Rescue an upset sailing canoe
Canoeing
    Paddle in wind and rough weather
    Paddle twenty miles
    Improvise sailing
    Make a canoe shelter
    Know the ways of handling a capsized canoe and demonstrate either pushing or splashing
Climb into a canoe from the water
    Paddle standing
    Final test
    Knots
    Tie bowline, eyesplice and whip end of a rope
Shafer
    Oral
    Written
    Practical – three minutes
    Count

The requirements for Water Queen were:

Swimming
    440 yards
    Three racing dives

Three running front dives
Five strokes
Tread water
Undressing test
Life Saving
Eight wrist holds
Three front strangles
Three back strangles
Ankle hold
Surprise hold
Three front wardings off
Three rear wardings off
Screenings
Three surface dives
Legs only – fifty yards
Arms only – fifty yards
Tired swimmer's carry
Shafer Method
Dock Work and Patrolling

In addition to the three water sports achievement levels, there were three levels of gypsy achievement levels called Little Gypsy, Gypsy, and Gypsy Queen. Requirements for achieving these levels involved camp craft, nature, farm work, and horseback riding. For example, Little Gypsy requirements were:

Camp Craft
    Walk forty miles – No distance less than five miles counts
    Roll poncho and make poncho bed or make poncho bed and roll it
    Make a good poncho shelter and sleep in it – Must be passed before and after
    Build tepee and log cabin fires using no more than three matches in lighting each
    Sleep out without talking from taps to reveille
    Be one of two cooks for a unit supper
    Be one of two wood gatherers and fire tenders for a unit supper
    Be able to use an axe properly
    Make a nature toy
    Make a cooking utensil
    Dress in a woodsy costume
    Nature

Twenty flowers including – Trailing arbutus, lady's slipper, sheep laurel, shineleaf, prince's pine, wintergreen, partridge berry, Trillium, and bunchberry

Fifteen trees

Ten ferns

Five birds – sight and song

Ten constellations – Know the difference between a star and a planet

Poison ivy

Kill fifty gypsy moths and larvae

Farm work

Work eight hours

Riding

Ride three hours

Bridle and saddle correctly

Mount and dismount

Clean saddle and bridle

Know names of all the horses

Count

Emily's July 4 letter to her parents read:

Wednesday

Dear Mother and Dad:

There were supposed to be "big doings" to-day, and nothing happened because the weather prevented – Worse luck!

I didn't go in for the eleven o'clock swim to-day after jewelry – (which I love) – because my side hurt me pretty badly. The nurse gave me some Calcium when I asked her for Kodeine [*sic*], but I guess they both mean the same.

I played tennis in the afternoon and got beaten 6–3 by an awfully cute girl – Nancy Smith. Then I beat Frances Laundon a "love" game which made me feel better.

We went over to Rookies Island for dinner (?), and just as we got back, one of the most <u>awful</u> storms I've ever seen burst. Gee, it was grand – Thunder, lightning, lots of rain, and big waves. It didn't last long tho. The new girls had to do their stunts to-nite too. I did one with three other girls It wasn't half bad, and it was loads of fun watching ten others.

Listen – I haven't gotten clear over my homesickness yet by a long shot, and I'm dying to hear from you – so if I don't get a letter in a day or two, I'll call you Long Distance – You wouldn't care, would you?

    Lots of love

    Emmy

P.S. My bathrobe just came, Mother Thanks loads.

On July 5, Emily wrote:

Friday morn (for Thursday)

Dear Mother and Dad:

    We had Sivad on the tennis court this morning so that we could be shown how to roll our ponchos. You see, the regular Thursday night trips began to-day.

    I spent the morning fixing my tent, poncho, and writing letters. Dad dear, my side has been hurting me pretty badly, so that I've had to drop out of quite a few things – Isn't there <u>anything</u> I can do for it?

    I was on the supper committee, so I left with two other girls, and we took the food with us. We camped out on the point, right near Bob McCurdy's home (?). Bob is one of the councilors, and she's awfully cute. We had Salmon Pea Wiggle, cocoa, bread, and fruit for dinner. It was awfully good, and I burnt myself on two fingers helping to get it ready – More fun!

    After dinner we sat out on the rocks and I watched the White Mountain Camps fireworks, which were shot off to-nite instead of last nite because of the rain Wednesday. When they stopped, we sat around the fire and told stories till we had to turn in. Then I had to crawl into my poncho, and I spent the nite trying to untangle myself – Oof!

    More to-morow, and please write me, cause if I don't get a letter before Tuesday morning, I'm going to telephone you – Honest!

    Lots of love

    Emmy

PLEASE

WRITE

On July 6, Emily's letter read:

Friday

Dear Mother and Dad:

Mother's letter came at a most opportune time. I was just beginning to bubble over because neither of you will write, but the letter cheered me up considerably [this letter does not survive]. I wish it would happen more often.

I'm having a marvelous time here. It's all so different, and there is so much to do. I don't know if I like it better than Wildwood though, or even as well – (though I'm glad I'm having the experience) – However, there is the one big objection to camp which I knew there would be – not enough freedom. By that I mean that not every one can go out in the canoes – (I can't till I'm a water witch –); a non descript [level below Water Baby] or water baby can't sail or aquaplane either – and a non-descript can't go out in a row boat without a water baby – that's all right if you get a nice water baby, but when you go on a trip and get a stubborn little twelve year old who think she knows it all in charge of your boat – well – I don't like it – and that's where Wildwood has it all over this.

This morning a man came and took our pictures and after that was over, I played a set of tennis with Nancy Smith – (the girl who beat me the other day) – and beat her 6–4 – whee!

After rest hour this afternoon, I went riding. I got a good horse and did a lot better, tho when I asked Johnny [Culbertson] – (the boy who helps the riding master) – whether I posted or bounced, he told me I did neither – so I guess I do a little worse than both – Gosh – what a life! But it's fun! I went in swimming when I came back – then I had dinner with the other Heavenlies on the rock opposite the bungalow – Gee camp's fun!

Please write soon –

<u>Gobs</u> of love

Emmy –

P.S. Halsey said Bud is getting along grand, in case the dear child hasn't written.

On July 7, Emily wrote:

Saturday

Dear Mother and Dad:

I had weaving this morning for the first time – It's more fun, and tho I can't make out exactly what I'm doing, I enjoy it loads. Makes me feel so industrious – I'm not going to tell you what I'm weaving – S'big secret so – "don't ask."

This afternoon the girls hiked into Casco. The girls that didn't want to walk, who were too lazy to, got to ride in the Migis [the name of a motor boat used by the camp]. Needless to see – I rode in the Migis. It was more fun. We got into South Casco way ahead of the hikers and got at the ice cream first. I ate twenty cents worth of chocolate, and two ten cent boxes of chocolate and vanilla. Gee it was good! I saw Bud. He looked dirty but cute, and seemed <u>quite</u> happy. Say, I'm being gyped – Since Bud gets the paper, why don't I? <u>Why</u>? Won't you please send it to me too. Lots of the girls here get a paper.

This evening we had classifications. That is, every girl is called up separately – (we had been weighed beforehand) – and Halsey and the nurse said whether we were "too thin," "tough," "regular," "too thick," or "husky." You're "too thin" if you're under weight and haven't much muscle. You're "tough" if you're underweight but muscular. "Regular" is not much over or under weight, and not an over amount of muscle. "Too thick" means too fat with not much muscle, and "husky" means overweight but muscular. I'm seven and a half pounds under, and was hoping against hope that I'd be classified as a "tough." That's the best thing to be, but I got "regular," and I'm so mad I could pop, and I'm going to be a "tough" before the summer is over if I possibly can.

There are northern lights to-nite, and they're simply gorgeous, so I think we'll be able to stay up later – here's hoping –

Please write soon –

Lots of love

Emmy

P.S. I'm off Skinny for life – He hasn't written me in three weeks, and besides, "Taps," our bugler, is much nicer –

More love.

Em –

On July 8, Emily wrote:

Sunday

Dear Mother and Dad:

To-day being Sunday nothing much happened. It was awfully hot, but I played tennis with Doris Benson for a little while in the morning. I had her 2–1 when we stopped because of the heat.

At Sivad this morning a man, Dr. Eppler, spoke to us on the

life of Clare Barton. It was interesting, but much too long, and the mosquitoes were terrible.

After rest hour, we had a dip – (incidently [Emily always spelled the word this way, instead of "incidentally"] "Taps" let us sleep almost half an hour too long). After supper, we – (that is the Heavenlies) – went out on Heavenly rock and learned a song to Hiiteni. Then we went to Sivad and fed the mosquitoes again while someone else talked to us till taps blew.

P.S Say hello to Kay for me, and tell her I'd write her but I can't remember her last name –

P.S. Camp is glorious!

[No signoff]

Emily's July 9 letter said:

Monday

Dear Mother and Dad:

I got Mother's two letters and the enclosed card this morning, and they made me feel great – I wish that many came every day – (Just a hint) – but really – it was grand [these letters do not survive].

I had weaving all day to-day. It was rather tiresome toward the end, but I like it. I think I'll finish what I'm making to-morrow morning – here's hoping anyhow.

Well, I've got a B.F. (best friend) – and she's a peach – You'd both love her – She's just the type you both like – Lots of fun, and a peachy all around girl. She's an accomplished musician – (plays the bugle, drum, and piano well) – and has a lovely voice. She's "pleasingly plump" – (and how!), and has an adorable face, disposition, and everything. Her name is Doris Benson. She's awfully popular, and she likes me as well as I do her – Yea! She's in Boulders Unit.

The Heavenly [head counselor] Frannie Cooper is darling. She's twenty, rather short, decidedly brunette and awfully cute. Everybody likes her. There are some darling girls in Heavenly, and I love the girls in my tent. The one I like best is Peggy Wade, an awfully cute, harum-scarum Syracuse girl who is a marvelous swimmer. Sue Miller, tent councilor, is lovely, and Mac Frothingham who is also new, is a cute little blond who is a lot of fun. Some of the other Heavenlies I like best are Betty [Eleanor] Bingham, whose side-kick is FannieBelle Allen. They're two of the most popular girls in camp. Dorothy Wilson and Babs [Dorothy] Van Duyn are also awfully cute. Frances Laundon is a Heavenlie too.

Hiiteni is still quite sick and can only see one or two girls a day. I haven't been able to meet her yet, but even though she is not around, we all sort of feel as tho she's there. I can't explain it, but the spirit here is glorious.

To-nite is council fire nite. It was much more serious than last week, and I liked that part better, [but] the count wasn't as good as the first one. The Timanous Pointers came over for council fire, and Mit said that Bud is carrying off all the honors and is certainly doing himself proud. I don't know just exactly what the honors were, but Bud will probably write and tell you – (at least I hope he will) – Please write soon.

Lots and lots of love
Emmy

On July 10, Emily wrote:

Tuesday
Dear Mother and Dad,

I got Dad's wire or whatever it was this morning, and it came just at the wrong time [this telegram from Dr. Sophian does not survive]. Peggy Smith, who is in charge of just about everything, and Sue Miller and Frannie Cooper all found out about it, and they won't let me "do things" now – I missed out on a hike to Raymond, which is twelve miles going and coming, just because of that telegram. Dad darling, won't you please write that I can do everything. My side is pretty bad, but then it has been off and on for over a year now and I hate to miss out on things, on account of it. There's so much always happening, and it's all so much fun. I wish you'd come up and see it. I never imagined camp could be like this, and I doubt if there are many, if any like it. Of course, I've never seen Hiawatha, but from what I know of Wohelo, and what I've heard of Miss "Rit's" camp fire from Elise and co., I'm so glad I came here. Camp is a wonderful experience anyhow, and I think that I'm at one of the best, if not <u>the</u> best one, in the U.S.A.

I finished my weaving this morning, and then played tennis for a little while – (I've forgotten with whom) – Then I went in swimming, but Sue made me get out before the others and wouldn't let me try to pass side stroke for water baby just on account of that wire. So please write and say everything is all right – please – !

I had more fun during rest hour with Peggy [Wade]. We organize a new form of amusement every day. But now Frannie made us promise we'd sleep, so I guess the fun stops. After rest hour I played two sets with Frances Laundon. Then she and I played doubles with Jane Shurmer, who is the swimming councilor and "Kink" (I don't know her real name) [Edith Longsdorf]. We were getting beatten [*sic*] when we had to stop to gather wood, cause we were on the supper comittee [Emily always spelled "committee" in this way—"comittee"] to-nite, and we cook supper every Tuesday evening [the cooks went to town that day for supplies]. Dotty Wilson, who was also on the comittee, didn't feel much like working – either did I. So we got the provisions – a thing which took us quite a while to do. Then when we didn't have anything else to do, we went looking for the guests. We found "them," the riding instructor, and Ray, the man who helps him, in the dining room – and they were supposed to eat with us. They told us they were so late they didn't think they were expected, and said that when they found some food under a basket in the dining room, they decided to eat there. They didn't know (or care) to whom it belonged. What they were eating looked lots better than what we were going to have, so when they asked us to join them, we did. Gee it was good! Then we all came back and had dinner with the rest of the unit. I also helped Dotty write a letter to her boy friend. It was more fun.

After dinner I played [word?] with "Taps." Before the game was half over, we had a huge audience. The few boys sure draw a mob around here.

Please write soon, and don't either of you work too hard. I certainly hope the heat lets up.

[No signoff]

Emily's July 11 letter read:

Wednesday
Dear Mother and Dad:

Big excitement to-day, some motion pictures men came to take pictures. We had regular schedule till bugle blew. I went to jewelry – then we all got into our bathing suits and went down to Lewa dock. Then they hitched up all the war canoes, and the regular canoes behind them, and attached the whole line of them to the Migis. A forward tow followed, and did I get tanned – gee it was great!

After two, there was an exhibition in the war canoes, and some lovely squad pictures. Johnny [Culbertson] took some or rather a great many pictures for me with my camera. I thought he could do it better than I could, because I couldn't focus anything. I hope they come out.

Nothing much happened this afternoon. It rained so Doris [Benson] brought her writing stuff up to my tent and we wrote letters while Peggy tried to distract us.

This evening we danced on the tennis court. It was a lot of fun, and since there were only three boys, or rather men, around – Bob, Johnny, and "Farmer Brown" – they got a big rush. They quite enjoyed the sensation of being "cut in on" by girls – at least "Farmer Brown" did – He's the only one I danced with. The other two are younger and cuter than he, and I didn't have quite enough nerve to ask them to dance. Better luck next time –

More to-morrow, when there's some new.

Loads of love

Emmy

P.S. Please take care of yourselves, please!

On July 12, Emily wrote:

Thursday

Dear Mother and Dad:

I went to pottery this morning and annoyed Betty Selkirk – who teaches it – that is, I didn't really annoy her, but I was feeling awfully silly, and you know me when I'm in a silly mood. Pottery didn't hold my attention long – it's rather uninteresting so I came back to my tent and rolled my poncho for the trip this evening. The Timanous boys were also going on a trip, so we hiked over there for the night. A truck took the girls who couldn't or who didn't want to walk – It's seven miles over there. Sue Miller and Frannie did their best to make me ride, but I fooled 'em and walked, tho it took some tall talking. We stopped in Casco for some ice cream, and incidently saw Bud there. Peggy Wade and I walked to-gether and had loads of fun. We stuck flowers in our hair and pretended we were Spanish dancers. Also, Peggy wanted to know whether men's beards grew after they were dead. More fun! We were all pretty hot and tired by the time we reached Timanous, so we all went in for dip. It (Panther Pond) isn't half as nice as Sebago, and Timanous can't compete with Wohelo, but we had loads of fun anyhow – not doing much – but – gee – Camp's Great!

Now for a nice cold nite with a sticky poncho and mosquitoes – more fun –

Best love
Emmy

Estelle wrote the following letter to Emily on July 12, 1928:

Thursday
Dearest Emmy:

Two letters to-day after the famine of yesterday –

I thought you knew that Buddy was to have the K.C. paper. He could not survive if he could not follow the sport news – As for you, you would be reading the story and I would like to feel that you are giving your eyes a rest –

Have you made any more attempts at becoming a "water baby" so that you could go in a row boat by yourself – Tough luck your being "regular." I think that is the best grade of all –

Had another séance with Mrs. Reineke this afternoon and let us hope with better results –

If you have time write to Miss Katy O'Connor, 2048 E. 12th Place, Tulsa, Oklahoma – I know it will cheer her to hear from you –

So far you have not written to Aunts Polly and Floey. Be sure to do so at once because they leave here next Wednesday –

I do not see why you complain about not receiving letters – I write nearly every day –

While I was gone this afternoon, James moved nearly the whole apartment. Another day or two and we shall be all set –

Much love to you from Mother

Dr. Gulick and other "physical culture" educators believed that the art of dancing was as important an element of physical education as any other. Drs. Dudley Sargent and Gulick agreed in a *New York Times* article, dated April 18, 1905, that rhythm was immensely important, because "it relieves the strain of work by making movement automatic, and does away with weariness." Dr.

Gulick wrote in *The Healthful Art of Dancing*, "Folk dancing is conducive to physical and moral health." He did not view folk-dancing "as a spectacle, but as a means of healthful recreation, of self-development and expression. ... Dancing is not only the most universal of the arts, but the mother of all art." He avowed that dancing is "the joy of life, the play of the world, that which makes us truly children of the spirit."[7]

On July 12, Estelle wrote:

> Dearest Emmy:
>
> I discovered your bathrobe a day or two after your departure and sent it to you addressed to Camp Wohelo as well as a letter. If you have not received them make inquiries accordingly.
>
> It makes us both very happy that you are so thoroughly enjoying your experience –
>
> We went to the club (Oakwood) after dinner last evening. A dance was in progress – All the jeunes filles [French for young girls] looked charming in their summery dance frocks – Louis was at a party Virginia Newhouse gave – His partner was Blanche Deutsch and since none of the other boys asked to dance with her he was saddled with her all evening – Aunt Gertie was not pleased –
>
> Your little friend Skinny (tout seul) was also there. He did not dance. At least I did not see him do so. He looked rather strange in a light blue blazer and white flannels. He did not see me – No letters have arrived or you would have had them –
>
> Your little brother was finally heard from. His letters were delayed – According to him he is the busiest person known and needless to say happy – Everything at his camp is fine and great –
>
> I hope you continue to have a good time. It seems strange to be here without you and rather lonesome. I feel certain however that you will be benefited by your experience – Has the pain in your side re-appeared? I hope not.
>
> This evening we are taking Mrs. Lehman out to dinner with us as her husband is still away and she is quite alone.
>
> Please write in greater detail.
>
> Heaps of love –
>
> Mother

Oakwood Country Club, mentioned above by Estelle in her letter to

Emily, was founded in 1881 in Kansas City by members of the Jewish Reform Congregation B'nai Jehudah as a place for social activities for the then fifty German-Jewish families.[9]

Emily's letter on July 13, 1928, said:

Friday

Dear Mother and Dad:

Had more fun this morning – We had pancakes for breakfast, and by the time they were ready, we were all starved. Peggy Wade and Doris woke Dotty and I up at ten of six. Peggy wanted to sing and Dorrie didn't want her to – Peggy sang – they fought – and we had to wake up and laugh. You know I've always loved pancakes but when they're eaten over an open fire after a night spent camping out – well –I couldn't [word?] at them quick enough and they only lasted four times around – Worse luck!

The girls who were walking back to camp left shortly after we cleaned up – the rest of us waited for the truck – and did we have fun! We tried to get a 1918 Ford started but it was locked, so we didn't have much luck. We (Dotty and Westie [Marion West]) therefore sat in it and waited. Pretty soon Bud, with some of the other boys, came back. We fooled around with Bud for awhile, then one of the councilors got in the Ford while some of the others pushed it out on the road. Just as it started, Dotty, Westie and I jumped for the running board. Dotty and I landed there but Westie missed it. The car was rolling so terribly that Dotty and I soon climbed into the front seat. Then Walt, the councilor, "stepped on it," and we bounced up the hill and back to camp again at a pretty fast rate – gee it was fun! We went once more, only this time, a bunch of the other girls climbed on too. When we got back, Babs Eaton was driving the cook's car around – (He had given her the keys) – so we piled in with her, and rode around for awhile. When we came back, we went inside and were entertained by a clog dance by one of the councilors. When he finished, Mr. Mis began to introduce the boys to us. First as he started to name the best one, our truck drove up, so we all made a mad dash for the door, without even looking or listening – Wonder what the boy felt like.

We had more fun on the way back – singing, yelling, and bouncing. When I got back here, there were two letters waiting for me. I was so glad to hear from Dad but, please don't fly to New

York – I'll be <u>awfully</u> worried in the first place, and in the second place who'll stay with Mother? Please don't fly if you can possibly help it. [The two letters do not survive.]

We had lunch at one, and then I slept till four, when I woke up after much effort to see the water witches off. They were leaving for the water witch trip on the Timanous house boat – Lucky bums – I don't know where they are going tho. When they had left, Peggy Smith [assistant director] went with me while I paddled one of the islands for water baby, and she taught me a different and more correct way of paddling. I forgot to tell you in my Wednesday letter that I passed one of my dives for water baby. I think I might have passed more, but the whistle blew for all out.

We had dinner on the dock – hoping that Bob would come back from Portland in time to take us out in the Migis – but he didn't, so I'm out in a row boat with Babs Eaton now, and we're writing letters. We're going to read later.

More to-morrow, and please take care of yourselves – I'm awfully sorry it's so hot.

All my love
Emmy
P.S. I forgot to tell you about the new "system" here – Whenever anyone's late to a meal, she has to stand up in front of the whole dining room and sing a song. The swimming staff is usually late, so they have made up a song which is beginning to get tiresome, but which is cute. You should hear some of the rare selections that are sung. What geniuses are hidden in this camp! I haven't been late yet tho –
More love –
Emmy –

Emily knew that her father, Dr. Abraham Sophian, had already made his first airplane trip less than three months earlier on April 22, 1928, by request of Tulsa, Oklahoma oil operator and cattle rancher Horace Greeley Barnard (1883–1970). Horace Barnard's son was ill at the Shattuck Military Academy in Faribault, Minnesota. Information about how Mr. Barnard knew Dr. Sophian is not available. Nevertheless, Mr. Barnard asked Dr. Sophian to fly to Faribault to assess his ill son and Dr. Sophian obliged.[10] The distance between Kansas City and Faribault is about 370 miles.

Biplanes were the only type of airplanes readily available in 1928, and

Dr. Sophian probably traveled to Faribault, Minnesota in a two-seater open-cockpit biplane called the "C3." The C-3 was built only in Tulsa, Oklahoma, between 1926 and 1928, by the Mid-Continent Aircraft Company. Tulsa oil baron William G. Skelly (1878–1957) purchased Mid-Continent in 1928 and changed its name to Spartan Aircraft Company. Skelly had migrated from his birthplace in Erie, Pennsylvania to El Dorado, Kansas in 1916, and then moved to Tulsa, Oklahoma in 1919, where he founded Skelly Oil Company. The Spartan Aircraft Company began to produce a monoplane (the Spartan C2-60) only in the 1930s, years after Dr. Sophian flew to Faribault. Skelly sold the company to J. Paul Getty (1892–1976) in 1935.

The length of the Spartan C3-165 was twenty-three feet; its span, thirty-two feet, and its height, eight feet, ten inches (Dr. Sophian was at least six feet tall.) Its maximum speed was 118 mph; its cruise speed, 100 mph; and its range, 600 miles. Its maximum weight at takeoff was 2,618 pounds and its useful load, 968 pounds (Dr. Sophian was thin).[11] Aircraft historian Rob Simpson wrote the following about the Spartan C3:

> The Spartan C3 was typical for the many new biplanes which appeared in the USA in the early prewar [pre-World War II] years. Originating as the Mid-Continent Spartan of 1926 and built by the Spartan Aircraft Co. of Tulsa, the initial C3-1 gained type approval in September 1928. … It was a tube, wood and fabric aircraft with two open cockpits accommodating three people, and the tail unit had a distinctive square shape. The Spartans were used by flying schools for instruction and by barnstorming companies. Only five Spartans are thought to have survived in the USA but at least two are currently airworthy.[12]

The Spartan C-3 flight that likely transported Dr. Sophian to Faribault seems to have originated in Tulsa, possibly with Horace Barnard and a pilot aboard, and flown to Kansas City (217 miles) where it refueled and picked up Dr. Sophian before heading north to Faribault. Dr. Sophian could have met the airplane at the New Richards Field (built and dedicated in 1927 by Charles Lindbergh [1902–1974]), which was quickly renamed Kansas City Municipal Airport.

The fledgling airplane industry experienced grisly biplane and monoplane crashes during the 1920s, and Emily's concern that her father might undertake flight between Kansas City and New York City is understandable. For example, a newspaper article dated Monday, August 1, 1927, reported a grim series of recent Midwestern airplane crashes.[13] The article noted that the first crash in Wichita, Kansas, involved two pilots, as follows:

> Artificial respiration administered by two nurses and an unidentified spectator, was credited today with having prevented Lieut. C. W. Luthy from choking to death a few moments after the plane in which he was making a return trip to Fort Riley crashed yesterday near the Wichita airport, killing Lieut. C. A. Pearson outright [Wichita is about 100 miles south of Fort Riley, Kansas].
>
> Luthy was removed from the demolished Curtiss "Jenny" airplane [the most famous World War I basic trainer], his nose and upper jaw crushed, his face lacerated badly and bleeding internally. He spent a "fair" night and hope is held for his recovery unless complications set in or it is found he is injured internally. The fliers came here with other members of the flying squadron from Fort Riley yesterday. They took off in the Curtiss [bi]plane and had ascended about 500 feet when the engine stalled and the plane took a nose dive.[13]

The second crash on August 1, 1927 was witnessed by 200 people who watched "a new Swallow monoplane carrying a pilot and two passengers plunge to the earth in flames" in New Castle, Indiana. "All of the occupants were killed and their bodies charred beyond recognition. The plane was piloted by Lieut. George Myers, of the reserve corps. With him were Paul Wise and Evan Davis, New Castle. The cause of the accident is unknown. The monoplane was said to be similar to that which crashed in Chicago Saturday, killing two men."[13]

The third crash, in Chicago, prompted a cry for a "city ordinance or state law making it compulsory for airplane owners to provide parachutes for pilots and passengers." On August 1, 1927, pilot George Zabriskie and student flier James Rose died when their plane caught fire. "Zabriskie was believed to have fallen from the machine when he crawled out on the wing to put out the fire with an extinguisher. Rose jumped from the flaming craft when it was 200 feet from the ground. Experts said lives of both would have been saved if they had had parachutes. The plane, owned by Zabriskie was a new machine."[13]

Meanwhile, another plane chartered at Chicago on August 1, 1927 by Mr. and Mrs. George T. Burrell, Jr. crashed on a journey to New Orleans. "The plane was forced to land in a corn field a few miles outside the city when the motor failed. It was too badly damaged in the landing to be repaired immediately." No one was hurt. Unfazed, the couple continued to their destination by automobile.[13]

A description of Dr. Sophian's experience flying in an airplane in 1928 is not available. However, since he was considering taking a second, more dangerous airplane trip (to New York City from Kansas City), his first trip must have thrilled him.

Emily's July 14, letter read:

Saturday
Dear Mother and Dad:
    It rained this morning, so nothing much happened. I slipped on the way to the mail box to get Mother's letter – (by the way, I don't see why you should complain – I've written every day, and long letters too) – and I did something to my wrist. I don't know just what, and the nurse doesn't either – (gosh she's dumb!) – but it hurt pretty badly and I can't use it, so I made her tape it for me. It feels better now. (Can you make any sense out all that? You're <u>pretty</u> good if you can.)
    I forgot to mention Leon's letter. It was stupid and I tore it up without reading it very thoroughly. He's <u>pretty</u> dumb!
    The girls hiked into South Casco this afternoon but I felt lazy, so I rode in on the truck with Betty Knowland. Ray is a pretty careful driver tho, so it wasn't much fun.
    I saw the baby brother in Casco. He looks great! He's awfully sunburned, and his hair is just one mass of curls, but the girls all think he's darling. I'm awfully proud of him!
    Not much news – so more to-morrow –
    Best love,
    Emmy

On July 15, Emily wrote:

Sunday
Dear Mother and Dad:
    "Taps", like a dumbbell, overslept this morning and didn't blow reveille, so we only had twenty minutes to take a dip and get in to breakfast. The camp was ready to murder him – He sure

deserved it! Sivad was extra long – to-day being Sunday, but it was awfully nice.

Nothing happened the rest of the day until four-thirty, when all the sisters [of boy campers at Timanous] and some other girls piled into the truck and went over to Timanous for supper and council fire. Gee we had fun! And we had chicken salad for dinner, and cake – Whee! Big treat! I sat at Ed Noyes table – He's a councilor. Bud sat on the other side of me, and Johnny Culbertson, from our camp was opposite me. It was fun.

Council fire was about an hour after supper and was I ever proud of Bud – I wish you could have been there. He got Water Wizard, Land Jester, Varsity Squad, Crow Shooter and Marksman. Halsey also got up and made a short speech about the "is." Voyagers comes after Woodsman, and it is a great honor to get into it, as it is purely honorary as is Woodsman – and only the very best all-around fellows are taken into it. Halsey said that it was very difficult to be worthy of it, but that the Voyagers were considering taking one or two boys into it very soon. I asked several boys later who they thought those boys would be and every one of the them said Bud. They also said that the Woodsman decided that they wanted Bud as one the very first days, and another boy told me that Bud was considered one of the finest boys in camp – Am I proud of him – Whee – and how. More to-morrow.

Bestest love

Emmy

Estelle wrote her daughter the following letter on July 15, 1928:

Dearest Emmy:

It is a pleasure to know that you are so very contented with your camp and find the girls so delightful. I would just love to be in your camp and meet the girls [you] admire but I fear that is not to be this year.

You see the Washington ranch is a definite [word?] and Daddy is afraid to go there and I can't be in both places.

We spent the last few days settling details and it has not been pleasant but the past is past and your Dad is satisfied so that's that.

Aunt Gertie's father died suddenly Tuesday morning and she wanted me to tell you that she had commenced a letter to you but of course has not been able to finish. I wish you would write her a nice letter suitable to the occasion as I am certain you know very well how to do.

So far Aunt Polly and Aunt Floey [Estelle's sisters] have not heard from you – I feel rather badly about it –

Yesterday, I received a very long letter from Mrs. Bush. They are enchanted with Wildwood and say it is the best they had seen.

We miss you a lot – Hope you continue to have a good time.
Loads of love
Mother
P.S. Katz wants to be remembered. Why not send her a card? Mother –

The Washington state transaction Estelle mentioned in her letter above to Emily was the purchase of a 6,000-acre ranch in northern Stevens County (county seat, Colville) in the extreme northeastern section of Washington state. Legal records described the Sophian purchase, as follows:

[T]he property consisted of some 600 acres of apple orchard with trees from 6 to 14 years old and bearing Spitzenburg, Rome Beauties, Jonathans, Delicious and Winesaps [apple varieties]; 300 acres of apple orchard of the same variety but not in as good condition; 400 acres of alfalfa land; 1000 acres all cleared; 3700 acres of timber and cut over land; pumping plant and irrigation system installed in 1923; various buildings, consisting of cold storage plant, apple warehouses; necessary machinery to harvest apples; a 27 room hotel; bunk house of 20 rooms and lobby with upper floor for apple storage; 9 cottages all plastered; 2 room school house; 3 machine sheds; blacksmith shop; machinery, tractors, tools and equipment, all of which furnished sufficient facilities to permit farming and horticulture on a large scale. The property and improvements were estimated by the owner, before acquisition by the [Sophians] to have cost and as of the value of $1,008,500.00.[14]

Abraham Sophian relished the experience of owning a huge working farm, and he bought and sold (always at a loss) at least three during his lifetime. The opportunity to own a 6,000-acre working farm in the untamed Far West, complete with a resort that his family could enjoy, must have been enticing. Vast irrigation projects funded by the National Reclamation Act (P.L. 57-161, 32 Stat. 388) of June 17, 1902 were rendering the arid land of the Far West agriculturally productive.[15] The National Reclamation Act was also known as the Newlands Reclamation Act after its author Democratic Representative Francis G. Newlands (1846–1917) from Nevada.

The irrigation initiatives expanded and diversified agriculture in many parts of the state of Washington. However, irrigated land became the most expensive farmland causing purchasing farmers to buy and cultivate relatively small tracts of land. They planted this land with apple orchards, rather than wheat, because apples earned the farmers substantial profits even on small orchards. A period of "apple fever" began around 1908 during which Washington farmers planted at least one million apple trees. By 1917, Washington was the leading producer of apples in the United States.[16]

The Upper Columbia River area of Stevens County, site of the Sophian ranch, was brought under irrigation and intense cultivation around 1910. The Upper Columbia River irrigation district extended almost to the international boundary line between Canada and the United States, as described in one report in 1910, as follows:

> The lands lie in a series of benches which originally were covered with a growth of pine and tamarack timber. Several tracts, totaling 15,000 acres of irrigable land, are being opened here by the Upper Columbia Company. The first unit of 1,500 acres is now nearing completion. The lands extend from a point several miles north of the town of Northport in a general southwesterly direction *to and some distance below the village of Marble* [emphasis added; Northport was seven miles upstream from Marble, site of the Sophian ranch]. The method of irrigation is by gravity flow, the water being secured from Deep creek, Crown creek, Sheep creek, Onion creek, and other tributaries of the Columbia river. The elevation varies from 1250 feet to 1750 feet.
>
> Apples have been raised in this section for years without irrigation, although the rainfall is not sufficient for maturing the fruit in perfect form. The soil is gravelly, with a liberal percentage of loam and volcanic ash, and fruit trees and all manner of vegetation grow very rapidly.[17]

Unfortunately, sulphur dioxide emissions released from a lead and zinc smelter in Trail, British Columbia, ten miles north of the international line between Canada and the United States, were moving down the Upper Columbia River valley, ruining farm land, forests, and crops. Abraham and

Estelle Sophian and other farmers in the Upper Columbia River region sought remedy from the Consolidated Mining & Smelting Company of Canada, Ltd., which had purchased the smelter from American owners and incorporated it as a subsidiary of the Canadian Pacific Railroad in 1906.[18]

Did Abraham and Estelle know about the Canadian smelter plant emissions when they purchased the 6,000-acre farm in 1928? Did they visit the farm before they purchased it? This information is not available. If, however, they possibly knew of the existence of an upstream smelter plant, they likely did not know that in 1925 and 1927 the plant's owners had increased its size and capacity to smelt zinc and lead ores and had installed two 400-foot smoke stacks. The increased capacity of the plant doubled the amount of sulfur emitted into the air from about 4,700 tons per month in 1924 to about 9,000 tons per month in 1927. Every ton of sulfur released into the air resulted in two tons of sulfur dioxide, which damaged the foliage of the forests, orchards, and crops. The sulfur dioxide was measurable in the rainfall.[18]

A group of Upper Columbia River farmers, including the Sophians, "succeeded in raising so much attention to their cause that the federal government took on their case. At one point even Democratic President Franklin D. Roosevelt [1882–1945, served 1933–1945] wrote the following letter to [Canada's Conservative Party] Prime Minister Richard Bennett [1870–1947, served 1930–1935]:

> I am receiving in increasing numbers protests from residents and officials in the State of Washington. These communications disturb me greatly and cause me to fear that, unless a way is found as soon as possible to reach a settlement of this case, real harm may be done to the relations of Canada and the United States in the Far West. The continuing drifting of sulfur dioxides into the State of Washington, with its consequent injury to the interest of a large number of American citizens, is a matter to which I cannot remain indifferent."[19]

Between 1928 and 1935, the US Government objected to the Canadian Government that sulfur dioxide emissions from the smelting operation in Trail, British Columbia, were causing damage to the Upper Columbia River valley in a thirty-mile stretch from the international boundary to Kettle Falls, Washington (including Marble and the Sophian's farm). On February 28, 1931, the International Joint Commission of the United States and Canada

(IJC-UC) decided that the Trail smelter plant should limit its sulfur dioxide emissions and that Canada should pay the United States US$350,000 as compensation for damages. During the next decade, the US Government paid damages of US$428,179.51 to settle all claims filed by individual property owners in Washington state against the Trail smelter.[20–21]

Historian Keith A. Murray summarized the historical importance of the Trail Smelter case, as follows:

The Trail Smelter Case of 1926 to 1934 is important in the study of United States-Canadian relations for two reasons. It was the first case of pollution to come before an international tribunal, and it was the first time that the Canadian government had complete control of the settlement of a problem by international arbitration, from original complaint to final settlement, without clearing its actions through London. Since the issue had no precedent in international law, and very few precedents in national law, the tribunal that examined the facts and rendered a judgment had little to go on; indeed it established a precedent subsequently used in other cases.[21]

The Sophian family was likely disappointed upon reaching its imagined paradise in the Upper Columbia River region in late August 1928, although no record of their reactions and experiences exists. Emily and Bud must have been especially appalled at the smells, stinging of their nasal mucosa, and sights of damaged orchards in the Upper Columbia River region after spending the previous seven weeks in the unspoiled beauty and cleanliness of Maine backcountry.

Emily wrote on July 16:

Monday
Dear Mother and Dad:
    I went riding after Sivad this morning with Peggy Wade, Mac Frothingham, Eleanor Vincent, Dotty Wilson, Johnny and Ray. I got a good horse, but a rather frisky one – I bounced more than was comfortable, and I was kinda scared when we cantered across the field. I wasn't very sure I could stick on. I did tho and had a lot of fun, but Mac fell off. She wasn't hurt at all, however.

Say Mother, I've wrecked two pair of stockings and I need six pair at least, so will you please send me four pair as soon as possible. And I need a couple of "bras," and two pair of pants – (more track pants) – Will you please get me some?

And Dad, I've got a favor to ask you. Frannie Cooper, our Head Councilor came in after taps last night, and said that she was going to write you and ask you what I could do , and what I couldn't. I finally talked her out of doing that, but she made me promise I'd stop "doing things" until you wrote and told me I could – so won't you write me a "special" and say that I can do everything – You see, it means no more hikes or horseback riding or anything for me till I hear from you, and I hate to miss it all.

My side has been hurting, but then that can't be helped, so please don't worry about it – I'm not.

How are both of you? I hope it isn't still hot in K.C., and if it is, I hope neither of you are working too hard – I'm worried – Honest. Are you still planning to go out West? I wish you would and I wish you'd leave soon if you possibly could – What about it?

Camp is great and I love it more every day. To-nite was council fire and we had about the best council fire yet. Gee it was great. I wish you could see one. They're really wonderful – serious and funny, impressive and entertaining.

Please write soon –

Best love

Emmy

P.S. What boat are Polly and Flo [Felix] sailing on and when do they sail. I want to write them on the boat.

On July 17, Emily wrote:

Tuesday

Dear Mother and Dad:

I was going to row one of my islands for water baby this morning, but I didn't feel very well, so Babs Eaton came up to the tent with me after Sivad, and read to me while I rested. I read and wrote letters this afternoon, so on the whole, it really wasn't a very eventful day.

This evening one of the girls played the piano and we danced on the tennis court. I had a lot of fun. I danced with Halsey quite a few times and he is a splendid dancer.

Sue Miller won't be back till late to-nite I don't think. All the H.C's and the swimming staff – (Sue is on the swimming staff) – went into Portland to see a movie. They went in specially to see the Fox and Pathé news pictures that were taken of our camp. Halsey said they came out marvelously. Be sure to see them if they come to K.C.

Please write soon

Bestest love

Emmy

P.S. I wrote Polly and Flo a special delivery letter to-day.

P.S.S. I don't see why you don't get a letter from me every day – I've written every day.

More love

Emmy

Pathé Brothers Company was founded in Paris in 1896 and rapidly became the largest film production and equipment company in the world. The company produced newsreels from 1910 until mid-1956 when newsreels in general ceased to be produced. The newsreels, which showed news, current affairs, and entertainment for millions of moviegoers, initially were theatrically silent with title cards describing the action on the screen. In the early 1930s, voiceover narration was added. Each newsreel usually contained anywhere from eight to fifteen clips of different stories. Apparently Wohelo camp was one of these stories.[22–23]

The news film (or one similar to it) that Emily mentioned in her letter has been preserved by the National Film Preservation Foundation and is available for viewing.[24] The Film Notes accompanying the silent film read:

"On the shores of Lake Sebago, Maine, dozens of radiant clear-eyed girls made the Luther Gulick camp, Wohelo, their own." So begins this promotional film about the pioneering all-girls summer camp founded by Dr. Luther Halsey Gulick and his wife Charlotte Vetter Gulick in 1907. The camps name, Wohelo, was coined by Charlotte from the first two letters of the words Work, Health, and Love, the three principles that inspired the Gulicks in their life long dedication to helping children and adolescents live "a well rounded life a vivid, intense life of joy and service."

The son of Congregationalist missionaries, Luther Gulick brought a near religious zeal to his interest in childhood development. By all accounts, he was a remarkable person:

founder of the YMCA Athletic League; Director of Physical Education in the New York Public Schools; and President of the Camp Fire Girls, which he established with his wife in 1910. Luther also designed the YMCA's triangular logo (symbolizing the interrelationship of body, mind, and spirit) and helped invent the game of basketball when he asked a young YMCA instructor to create an indoor sport emphasizing teamwork.

Charlotte Gulick was no less remarkable. She was the driving force behind Camp Wohelo, which grew from a family camp that she and her husband had started in Connecticut. Charlotte ran the camp and designed the educational programs that would later become an essential component of the Gulicks work with the Camp Fire Girls. When the family camp outgrew its grounds, Charlotte decided to establish a summer camp in Maine: Wohelo.

But although it delivered, as the films first title card says, "an intensive course of outdoor work," Wohelo was a camp with an educational mission. The film shows that fun was an important aspect of the curriculum. We see the girls involved in a wide range of activities, from jewelry making and pottery to canoeing, gardening, and horseback riding. While watching Charlotte Gulick start a fire without matches may remind viewers today of the trials and tribulations of *Survivor* [an American "reality" television game show that premiered on May 31, 2000 on CBS, an American television network], Camp Wohelo was definitely not an exercise in survivalism. Constantly foregrounded are the principles of play and cooperation, best exemplified by the scene of a group of girls making a synchronized backwards dive off of their canoe. As the title card reminds, it is "the spirit of camaraderie that makes for perfect teamwork."

Today, we may take organizations like Camp Fire and Girls Scouts for granted, but back in the early 1910s before the ratification in 1920 of the Nineteenth Amendment, which gave women the right to vote, the creation of all-girl camps was a revolutionary development towards equality of the sexes. While Luther Gulick sometimes gets the lion's share of credit for founding Camp Fire Girls, the film suggests that he was, in the words of a title card describing a scene of Charlotte Gulick holding a boy toddler, "one small warrior in a camp of Amazons." *Wohelo Camp*, filmed a year after Luther's death, is a fascinating tribute to the pioneering organization that preceded Camp Fire and to its matriarch

Charlotte Vetter Gulick and her "Amazon" girls, "hard as nails and dipped in sunshine."[24]

On July 18, 1928, Emmy wrote:

Wednesday
Dear Mother and Dad:

Half the camp went to the ocean to-day, so of course there wasn't much for the other half to do – I wrote the "girls" [Pauline and Flora, Estelle's older sisters] a special delivery letter to-day after I got Mother's letter. I'm sorry I didn't write them sooner, but I haven't had time. You don't realize how busy we are here.

I hate to make this such a short note, but I'll write a long one to-morrow after the other half – (including me) – comes back from the ocean – Please write soon, and take care of yourselves –

Bestest love
Emmy

Around July 17, 1928, Estelle wrote:

Dearest Emmy:

Funny you think I have been finding fault with your not writing – Such has not been my intention – when a day goes by and I do not hear from you, it makes the separation just a bit harder to bear. You have been very faithful and your letters have been a constant joy to me. Hence when a day goes by and I do not hear from you I have a sense of loss –

Buddy told me he lent you some money. Why did you not write to say you needed some although I believe you were rather extravagant if you spent all we had given you – I rather imagine you did not have enough with you that particular day but am enclosing a bill in the event you are short –

The final moving is being done to-day and although James has done remarkably well, a great deal still remains to be done – I am going down to Dad's office in a little while and I know by this evening James will have things looking fairly straight

I hope there is nothing seriously wrong with your wrist – Please don't get yourself all banged up –

Daddy is trying to arrange matters so that you and Bud can join us at the ranch – It means touring back, you know, as Dad and I plan to motor up there.

Heaps of love
Mother.

Motoring from Kansas City to Spokane, Washington in 1928 was an arduous undertaking. "Thru routes" (as opposed to secondary or main connecting roads) in Kansas, Nebraska, Wyoming, South Dakota, Idaho and Washington were almost all "improved roads", which was one level lower than "paved roads" and one level higher than ""graded roads." In a few areas, the thru routes were still "dirt or poor roads," according to the 1927 edition of *Rand McNally & Company Auto Road Atlas of the United States and Ontario, Quebec, and the Maritime Provinces of Canada* (Chicago, Illinois: Rand McNally & Company, 1927). Between Friday, August 10 and Thursday, August 16, 1928 (seven days on the road) Estelle and Abraham drove their Buick over approximately 1,600 miles between Kansas City and Spokane. This calculates to an average of around 230 miles per day or an average speed of around 30 miles per hour (if they motored eight hours per day) or 20 miles per hour (if they motored ten hours per day).

Emily's next letter was on July 19, 1928, as follows:

Thursday
Dear Mother and Dad:
I went to the ocean to-day – gee it was fun! It took us a little over an hour to get there, and I had lots of fun on the way. I went in a dilapidated Cadillac with Betty Bingham, Sue Miller, Mary Frances Wood, Lois Ashley, Julie Denison, and Eleanor Vincent – a nice bunch of "kids" (Betty and Julie are about eighteen or nineteen) – It was grand. We didn't travel at any snail's pace – neither did we miss a bump – and the way we hit them was "nobody's business" – It was fun.
We got into our bathing suits as soon as we reached Higgins Beach – our destination. Then, when we were all ready, we went in. The water was icy but marvelous and I loved it. We were only allowed to stay in about ten minutes at a time – but we went in twice in the morning and once in the afternoon – We stayed in our bathing suits all day and I got a gorgeous tan. I'm awfully brown now. Gee I'm glad! We had relay races and baseball games – incidently Heavenlies got beaten. Some of the girls stood on their hands and heads and did other tumbling stunts – I didn't do much of that tho.
We had clam chowder, crackers, punch and watermelon – and

I never ate so much in my life – I'm gaining pretty much – (too much) – I'll be fat soon – [Emily sketched in the margin of her letter one thin "stick figure" and one fat "stick figure"]

After lunch we just played around some more, and went shopping. I bought a little girl – (I don't know her name, but she was awfully cute) – a king-sized candy bar. Consequently she followed me around till I left. I also bought a balsam pillow for our tent besides "sump'n" that I bought for you and which I am sending to-morrow. [Maine balsam pillows are filled with the sweet-smelling needles of the Maine Balsam Fir Tree.]

I got Dad's letter when I got home. I was so glad to hear from him – it happens so rarely. Gee I'm glad the ranch is finally ours. Bud and I are both looking forward a lot to going out there – I can hardly wait – tho I'll be sorry to leave camp. When are you two going to leave K.C. [Kansas City]?

Please write soon and take care of yourselves –
Best love
Emmy

On July 19, 1928, Emily received a letter written in French from Sister Marie Emmanuel de Sion and Notre Mère Irene of Emily's school—the French Academy of Notre Dame de Sion in Kansas City. Sister Emmanuel thanked Emily for her letter of the previous Thursday, which gave great pleasure to Notre Mère, who, not able to thank Emily herself, said Sister Emmanuel, asked Sister Emmanuel to tell Emily that all the details she provided about camp were extremely interesting. Sister Emmanuel told Emily that even as all her little companions at camp are charming, she hoped that Emily was, among all of them, the most genteel, to give honor to Sion. After relating some information about the activities of familiar people to Emily at Sion, Sister Emmanuel told Emily to tell her friend who desired to attend the French Academy that the sisters of Notre Dame de Sion would receive her with open arms and much friendship. Sister Emmanuel asked for the girl's name and class, whether she spoke French, and where she lived. Sister Emmanuel expressed her deep affection for Emily, as did Notre Mère. Notre Mère wrote in her brief note at the end of the letter that Emily's writing brought her great pleasure, especially as they came from "her Emily" ("mon Emilie"). She signed, "All my affection to my great child. Notre Mère."

Emily's letter to her parents on July 20, 1928, read:

Friday

Dear Mother and Dad:

I got Mother's letter this morning and was surprised and shocked to hear about the death of Aunt Gertie's father – Gee, it's a shame, and I wish you'd tell her how sorry I am about it, but really, I just couldn't write her. I'd be sure to say the wrong thing.

It rained this morning so I went in Emily Jane Wood's tent and we wrote letters to-gether till lunch – Neither of us went in swimming – It was too cold and dreary, and besides, I'm not doing anything until I hear from Dad – Frannie won't let me – So I wish Dad would write soon.

I went up to the farm with Babs Van Duyn after rest hour this afternoon to pick flowers for Hiiteni. Say, did I tell you that I met her about a week and a half ago? Gee – she's marvelous. It's terrible to see how thin and emaciated she is – I'm afraid she's just wasting away, but gosh her spirit is marvelous.

We went to Rookies Island for dinner to-nite and had a marshmallow roast afterward. We stayed there till the White Mountain boys began to circle the island in canoes and made bright cracks – Then we left singing: "We own the lake" and the "Vulgar" Boatman song: 'More to-morrow.

Please write

Bestest love and take care of yourselves

Emmy

Around July 20, 1928, Estelle wrote to Emily:

Dearest Emmy:

Have you heard from Lucile [Emily's cousin] or have you written her? Aunt Jane [Felix-Sophian] wrote me, she sent you and Buddy some saltwater taffy – Be sure to write and thank her. I think it was very thoughtful of her because she did not know it was against camp regulations to send candy –

I am glad Buddy is doing himself and us proud by his conduct – I am sure you must have had a pleasant evening at his camp.

It is again very warm here. I had to go to town to-day to attend to a number of things and the city was like a furnace –

I am very tired now so more to-morrow.

Much love Mother.

Emily next wrote to her parents two days later, on July 23, 1928. On the back of the envelope in which she sent this letter, Emily wrote, "Have you gotten that package I sent you yet?"

Monday Morn.

Dear Mother and Dad:

I'm sorry I couldn't write Saturday or Sunday, but my iron constitution did me dirt and I've been kinda sick – nothing more than a stomach ache plus a pretty bad headache, but was in bed. The girls were adorable. Saturday night Doris Benson and FannieBelle Allen came up after all the others had left – (Bob McCurdy read to me almost all evening, and a whole bunch of girls were here) – and Doris rubbed my back while FannieBelle rubbed my head – Service, wasn't it? Gee they were darling. Altho Doris had to leave at Taps, Fannie stayed quite a while after – (she's a councilor).

I didn't go to Sivad yesterday morning, but I did go to lunch – It was the first time I'd eaten since lunch on Saturday – Woof! I slept almost an hour over rest hour, then I got up and went to watch Jane Schurmer – (the swimming councilor) – cut some of the girls' hair – She's quite good, and if I weren't letting my hair grow, I'd have her cut it for me – I might anyhow just for the heck of it.

It rained cats and dogs last night but we went over to Sivad and "got read to" anyhow. Peggy Wade, Dorrie Benson and I came back to-gether. Dorrie was the only one who had a flashlight, and was also the only one who missed the puddles – so Peggy and I fooled her and borrowed Rastus Chapman's light (Rastus is a senior councilor and a peach of a girl – I like her heaps, but I'm kind of in awe of her) –

We left Dorrie at Boulders, then we slipped and "slided" up Boulder hill – Gee were we soaking when we reached our tent – Ow!

I meant to tell you that I received a big box of taffy from Asbury Park, N.J. Friday. There was no card in it or anything, but I imagine that it was from Lou and her mother – Incidently I haven't heard from either of them – I'm awfully glad Lou got asked to be Princess of the [word?] Parade. Tell her so for me if you write her, will you? Did her Dad let her accept?

I've got such a collection of "stuff" from the girls in the short time that I've been here that I feel almost like a gold-digger – honest. I like it tho – Listen to this: I have Betty Bingham's ring;

Doris Benson's bracelet; Emily Jane Wood's pin; FannieBelle Allen's wrist strap; and Eleanor Bingham's little "chocolate drop" cupie – Isn't that great? Whee!

I hope you two don't think that just because I rave on about everyone and everything that I don't miss you – I do terribly – but then as long as I'm here, I'm having the best time I can – and that's an awfully good one. I'm awfully glad I'm here, but I'm also looking forward to and counting ten days till I'll see you again – That sounds <u>rather</u> mixed up and senseless, I'm afraid, but it's all true.

More to-nite.

Best love

Emmy –

P.S. When are you leaving for the ranch? I'm looking forward very much to going out there – so is Bud, and I <u>know</u> it will be <u>perfectly</u> all right for us to travel out there alone – Honest – I doubt very much if any councilor goes any farther west.

More love –

On July 24, Emily's letter was brief:

Tuesday Morn.

Dear Mother and Dad:

I've only got a second in which to say hello. We're leaving on the Crooked River [canoe] trip all of a sudden and everything is all messed up. You won't hear from me for about 3 days – I'm sorry –

Bestest love

Emmy

P.S. Thanks gobs for the dollar –

Crooked River is a tributary of the famed Songo River. Songo River is the "crookedest of all rivers" and is the chief connecting stream between Sebago Lake, Long Lake, and a chain of small lakes to the north.[25] The Songo empties into Sebago Lake's northern aspect about three and one-half miles northwest of Wohelo. One observer described the Songo River experience from the perspective of one entering the river from Sebago Lake, crossing the famous Songo sandbar, and thence moving upstream, as follows:

Crossing the "bar," [a boat] enters the mouth of that *one* river of Maine in *romantic* interest, the Songo, and threads her tortuous way up what is termed the "crookedest of all rivers. Songo is likewise of Indian origin signifying "The Outlet." It is but two and a half miles as the bird flies, to the head of the river, and yet we must sail six miles and make twenty-seven turns in traversing this singularly crooked stream, and are often within leaping distance of the banks. The passage up the narrow and sweetly sinuous Songo is the most interesting part of the trip, and its best feature is the direct reflection which the forest and banks make in the sluggish and tranquil stream. The most vivid colors and the most delicate foliage are duplicated in the dark mirror of the waters with marvelous accuracy.

After five miles' sailing and turning we reach the picturesque "Lock," at the confluence of Songo and Crooked Rivers. Soon after the settlement of the town of Gorham, one of the most formidable assaults on the English ever known in the early annals of Maine was made by the tribes from the interior.[26]

Henry Wadsworth Longfellow (1807–1882) wrote the following poem about Songo River on September 18, 1875, after a visit to the river in the summer then closing:

Nowhere such a devious stream,
Save in fancy or in dream,
Windy slow through bush and brake,
Links together lake and lake.

Walled with woods or sandy shelf,
Ever doubling on itself,
Flows that stream, so still and slow,
That it hardly seems to flow.

Never errant knight of old,
Lost in woodland or on wold,
Such a winding path pursued
Through the sylvan solitude.

Never school-boy in his quest
After hazel-nut or nest,
Through the forest in and out
Wandered loitering thus about.

In the mirror of its tide
Tangled thickets on each side
Hang inverted, and between
Floating cloud or sky serene.

Swift or swallow on the wing
Seems the only living thing,
Or the loon, that laughs and flies
Down to those reflected skies.

Silent stream ! thy Indian name
Unfamiliar is to fame ;
For thou hidest here alone,
Well content to be unknown.

But thy tranquil waters teach
Wisdom deep as human speech,
Moving without haste or noise
In unbroken equipoise.

Though thou turnest no busy mill,
And art ever calm and still,
Even thy silence seems to say
To the traveler on his way: –

"Traveller, hurrying from the heat
Of the city, stay thy feet!
Rest awhile, nor longer waste
Life with inconsiderate haste!

"Be not like a stream that brawls
Loud with shallow waterfalls,
But in quiet self-control
Link together soul and soul."[27]

Longfellow was born in Portland, Maine and, like Nathaniel Hawthorne, attended Bowdoin College. His most famous poems include *Paul Revere's Ride*, *The Courtship of Miles Standish*, *Tales of a Wayside Inn*, and the *Song of Hiawatha*.[28]

Crooked River is about five and one-half miles upstream from the mouth of the Songo on Sebago Lake and enters the Songo River on the right, from the perspective of a boatman moving upstream. Crooked River has many sets of rapids, which some of the Wohelo girls were permitted to ride in their canoes.

Emily's next letter was on July 27 (three days later), penned upon her return from Crooked River:

> Friday
> Dear Mother and Dad:
> We got back from the Crooked River trip just in time for lunch to-day. After lunch we had rest hour and I slept till the bugle blew for supper. At present it's raining, and the girls are dancing and making a lot of noise over at Sivad. I'm going to try to make up for lost time and try to give you an idea of what happened this week – so prepare yourself for a manuscript – (written incidently with the help of my flashlight, whose batteries are so run down that the blooming thing is worse than nothing. I'm going to try to get some more batteries next time I go to Casco – which means to-morrow) –
> Before I start on the news, I want to tell you that I'm so excited at the prospect of going west after camp, that I can hardly see straight – Gee I'm glad!! I half killed the girl I was with when I got Dad's letter yesterday [while on the Crooked River canoe trip] and found out that Bud and I would be allowed to travel out there alone – (They brought us the mail and supplies every day) – I bet Bud is even more thrilled tho if such a thing is possible. I don't know just exactly when camp is out or any of the details but I'll find out and let you know to-morrow.
> I got Mother's letter and the stuff this morning when I got back. Thanks ever so much – I'm just wild about the shorts and hate to cover them up with my bloomers – Pretty bad isn't it! I'm so sorry to hear that Doctor [name?] is worse, but I'll be so glad to see you if you could possibly come up, Mother. And if Dad went to N.Y. to see Dr. [name?], couldn't he come up here for about a day also? How about it Dad, it's only an overnight trip, and I want you to see camp and meet the girls – It's all too wonderful Not to mention the fact that I'm simply <u>dying</u> to see you both.

Monday [Emily continued her letter on the same sheet of paper on Monday, July 30] –

Nothing much happened except council fire in the evening. Timanous – (part of it) – came over for it, and Bud was here. Council fire lasted pretty late tho, and so I didn't get to see him afterwards – Gee I was mad.

Tuesday –

I sent you a scrawl just before we left for the trip in the morning – Could you make anything out of it? I'm awfully sorry not to have been able to write during the last few days, but I really couldn't help it. I won't miss again tho.

We left camp at about eleven thirty and the Migis towed us across Sebago and up the Songo River to the Songa locks. The two took a little over an hour, then we started to paddle up Crooked River and after about three quarters an hour, we stopped and ate. Then we started on again and paddled all afternoon. I was in a war canoe, because I'm only a non-descript, but even so I had fun. We sang and made lots of noise – more fun! Also, we passed several other camps who were also on canoe trips. Gee, did some of those little boys think they were "the berries" making all these wise cracks! You should have heard them! Some were really funny tho and it took a lot of self control to keep from laughing. We arrived at our destination – some ground that belongs to Hiiteni – at almost six o'clock. We unrolled our ponchos right away so that they would be ready for us later. I put mine with Doris Benson, Peggy Wade, Jannie Smith and Bob [Barbara] Lewis. FannieBelle Allen and Betty Bingham made a poncho shelter right near us.

After dinner, the real fun began tho – Gee I never laughed so much before – There was "Barber Shop" for some of the new girls. How I happened not to be chosen I don't know, but anyhow, they missed me and I'm sure glad they did. Here's what it is: The new girls are brought in one at a time and are placed on a box right near the fire. Bob Hertzler (who is one of the most amusing "boys" – he's twenty – I've ever met) was barber, and "Sly" manicurist. Bob put towels over the girl's middy and over her bloomers, around her neck, and over her eyes. Then "Sly" took her hands, and then they (Bob and Sly) began filling her with a lot of baloney about breaking an egg over her head. Then while they were talking, Jane Shurmer would sneak up, put her arms around the girl and kiss her. The girls of course all thought it was Bob, and some of the expressions on their faces were rare! Gee it was screaming! They saved Jean Baldwin, an awful fool, for the end. You see, Bob had to really kiss the last one. Well, I've never seen anyone go thru all the contortions Bob did before kissing her – he even tried to blindfold himself, but she didn't know that, and was thrilled to death and sat gazing rapturously into the fire the rest of the evening tho I thought that Bob had her saved specially for the end. Oof! What a pill!

When "Barber Shop" was over, Phil [Phyllis] and Molly Radford sang some darling songs – Oh I forgot. Johnny Culbertson was the last one to get "barbered," and he asked to be allowed to choose his own barber. They let him have Molly, so he was happy. She asked him whether he wanted a shave or a haircut. He chose the latter – Then they blindfolded him, and "Taps" kissed him, while Molly held him. He didn't know tho, so when they removed the blindfold, he asked Molly for a shave – They're a darling couple. Taps just blew so I'll have to write up Wednesday and Thursday to-morrow morning. I'm going to try to get it off by the first mail.

Wednesday
(next morning)

I just came back from the largest funniest and best Sivad we've had this summer. More has happened this morning, but I'll write you about it this evening in another letter, and continue writing about the Crooked River trip.

We had pancakes for breakfast Wed. morning and they were cooked over an open fire and were they good – Whoopee! I just ate and ate and ate – So did everyone. But the batter finally gave out. After breakfast we fixed our poncho beds, then I went up to the farm with Dorrie to get some water. It was pretty far and I got awfully tired so that when we got half way back, and we met Frannie Cooper, she made someone else take the water. It made me mad 'cause I hate being treated like an invalid. And I want to start working for water baby again. I'm awfully ashamed about not being one already. Can't I start in again? And I want to start riding again, so that I'll really know how when I go out to the ranch – Won't you write and say it's all right? Please some of the girls paddled up the river and shot the rapids in the afternoon. I didn't go tho. I stayed "in camp" with a bunch of girls and we went in swimming à la Adam and Eve.

After dinner, "Marty" Hedden (one of the Head Councilors) and I decided that we wanted to sing songs. We did for awhile, but the other girls didn't really appreciate our talent, so we proceeded over to the big fire and watched the entertainment. It was really very cute. Sue Miller got up and recited some simply adorable poetry – She was precious. Then some of the girls and councilors sang, recited and did stunts until we had to turn in. Then the fun began for Dorrie, Peggy, Janice, Bob, and I. During the day we had decided to make a canoe shelter, so we got a canoe, and took our ponchos off our blankets. We put two of them under us, and were going to attach three of them to the canoe for our shelter. Then we changed our minds and removed the canoe, and just spread the three ponchos over us. Well when we got into bed, we began to fight over the ponchos – about which one had the most, until we decided to make our beds over. It was way after taps tho, so we thought better of our decision, and spent the time laughing and quarreling instead.

Thursday

We had pancakes for breakfast again this morning and I ate more than the day before. They never taste this good at home. After breakfast most of the girls decided to go up the river and take their lunch. I was going up with FannieBelle, but she wasn't feeling very well, so in spite of the fact that she was willing to take me, I didn't go. Instead Debby Durstine and I, having nothing better to do, went up to the farm to get water. We took our own sweet time tho, as that by the time we got the water as far as the place where Frannie and some of the other H.C.'s had their ponchos, it was almost warm. The truck drove up just about then with "Sly" and the supplies – also with a book for me. Frannie came up then too, and she made "Taps," who also came in the truck, carry the water. I put up a pretty good argument, but it didn't do any good. "Taps" carried the water, and Debby and I stayed and talked.

In the afternoon, we had rest hour for over an hour and a half. Then we went in swimming à la natural again. We had an emergency all out because Halsey and Bob arrived on the truck and were liable to appear on the scene any minute – Was there every a scramble! Whoopee!

I was on supper committee – We had salmon cakes, toast, and fried potatoes. Wayne and Emily, the colored cooks here, sent over a gorgeous chocolate cake. The "cooks" got three helpings – Whee!

The entertainment was riotous. The girls got up and put on some of the stupidest one set plays I've ever seen, but one couldn't help laughing. FannieBelle Allen was a scream. She played the part of the ball and chain of a criminal in one, a newspaper in another, the scenery in a third, and a suitcase in the last. She's just adorable, and so I got a big thrill when she asked me to come into her poncho shelter and talk with her after taps. You see, Betty Bingham, who is a councilor, went to a dance with some of the H.C.'s so FannieBelle was alone. She was just adorable to me and I'm simply nuts over her, and I think she likes me pretty well, too.

Gee some of the girls envied me – more fun. I have to stop because I have no more paper, so I'll tell you about the trip home in to-nite's letter.

Take care of yourselves –
Loads and loads of love
Emmy

While Emily was writing the long letter above to her parents, Peggy Smith mailed to Estelle and Abraham and all the other parents or guardians of Wohelo campers a two-paged typed letter postmarked in Maine on Saturday, July 28, 1928. It read:

Dear Parents: –

Although surrounded by the beauties of nature and miles away from the whir of the bustling city, we at Wohelo are faced with the realities of life. As you undoubtedly have read in the press or been informed through friends, Hiiteni, a name dear to every girl who has ever been at Wohelo, but to the greater world and perhaps to you parents we better say, Mrs. Gulick, passed away at camp today.

The head and senior counsellors [sic] who have been brought up in the spirit of Wohelo for summers past, some of whom have started at camp as girls of ten or twelve, realize that Hiiteni's spirit will permeate this spot of beauty forever. The ideals and principles for which she has striven her entire life to make permanent are more alive than ever. No sadness or sorrow can exist at Wohelo and never will. Our activities and camp life are continuing as full of the spirit of fun and laughter as ever before and although the loss may seem depressing to the outside world we here at camp are seeing far beyond that, we are living Hiiteni's spirit of happiness and more abundant life. Her spirit is with us and will continue to guide through every day.

We are having a simple memorial service for the girls which will be full of beauty and the joy of life as she would wish. The spirit here will be more joyful and thoughtful than ever before and we earnestly desire that every girl will derive a deeper understanding of the joyousness and value of life through this experience.

I know you will understand and assist us in any immediate way, in making this summer as full of inspiration as any that have gone before.

Most sincerely yours
"Peggy" Smith
Assistant Director,
Sebago Wohelo

A *New York Times* obituary about Mrs. Gulick's death, dated Sunday, July 29, 1928, was titled, "Mrs. C. Gulick Dies in Camp in Maine; Founder of Campfire Girls of America Succumbs at 62 After a Long Illness; WAS WIDOW OF EDUCATOR [*sic*, capitals]; Devoted Many Years to Practice of Harmonious Development of Spirit, Mind and Body." The text of the obituary was:

Mrs. Charlotte V. Gulick, founder of the Campfire Girls of America and Director of the Luther Gulick Camps, died this morning in her Summer camp at South Casco, Me., after a long illness, at the age of 62. Her husband, Dr. Luther H. Gulick, educator, author and authority on hygiene and physical training, died ten years ago. She is survived by several children, one of whom, J. Halsey Gulick, will carry on the Luther Gulick Camps, assisted by Miss Marguerite Smith and Mr. and Mrs. Robert Boyden. Funeral services will be held at the Old South Church in Springfield, Mass., at 4 P. M. Monday.

Mrs. Gulick was born in Oberlin, Ohio, a daughter of the Rev. John Vetter. Following her graduation from Drury College she spent a year at Wellesley, and following her marriage to Dr. Gulick in 1887 she studied medicine for a year in order to aid her husband in his contemplated work as a medical missionary. They abandoned this purpose, however, settled in Springfield, Mass. and thereafter devoted themselves to teaching and practicing their educational principle of harmonious development of the spirit, mind and body.

In a Summer camp that she established in Connecticut Mrs. Gulick worked out many of the methods of training of youth that were used later by her husband as President of the Playground Association of America [and] as Director of the Department of child hygiene of the Russell Sage Foundation. At South Casco, Me., Mrs. Gulick realized her camp ideals at Camp Wohelo. The name was coined by Mrs. Gulick. It combines the first two letters of the three words that stand for the cardinal principles of Campfire, work, health and love. After the death of her husband Camp Wohelo became the Luther Gulick Camps, as a memorial to him.

The idea of the Campfire Girls originated with Mrs. Gulick and the enterprise was launched in 1912. From a small group of girls, it grew rapidly. There are now 170,000 active members and in the sixteen years of its history there have been 700,000 members. Dr. Gulick shared his wife's belief in the Campfire purpose, worked with her for its success, and for several years was President of Campfire. Mrs. Gulick edited the literature that fostered the movement and in many and various ways aided its expansion.

Mrs. Gulick was the first President of the Association of Directors of Girls' Camps. She belonged to the National Arts Club of this city, the Washington Arts Club, Twentieth Century Club and Women's City Club of Boston, and the Appalachian Mountain Club. In the World War she and her husband went to France on a mission for the Y. M. C. A.

Emily's July 29, 1928, letter to her parents read:

Saturday

Dear Mother and Dad:

This has been one of the strangest days I've ever spent – so much happened, and if I've ever said before that I admired the spirit of this camp, I don't know what I was talking about, because I don't believe I ever fully realized till to-day what it really is. It's too wonderful to put in writing – it's just too – well listen to this and see if you don't agree with me. I'm going to try to give you a complete picture of to-day – then maybe you'll be able to understand a little how perfectly splendid this place is.

When we got to breakfast this morning, Frannie Cooper stood up and said that she wanted to see all the old Heavenlies on the porch after the meal. That of course meant that Heavenly initiation is beginning – and it did. The trouble begins with the punishing of all the girls who aren't old Heavenlies and who have gone thru Heavenly gate. "Red" [Mary] Holmes was the first victim. She was asked to get up and make a three minute talk on sprained ankles. Well, "Red" got up and couldn't think of anything to say, so she stuttered around a little and sat down. Sue Miller was called on next to sing "I love Me." She made a brave attempt and the girls all clapped when she sat down. Then Babs Van Duyn was asked to give a three minute talk on "Why Fleas Leave Home." She got up and looked around rather vacantly, so they gave her till lunch to prepare it.

After breakfast I <u>helped</u> Babs write it out. Then we went to Sivad. It was one of the funniest and noisiest of the year. Everyone was feeling silly and acting up. When I came back I wrote, or rather finished that long letter to you. Then FannieBelle asked me up to her tent and we stayed there till just before lunch when word was passed around that we were all wanted in the craft house. When we got there, Peggy Smith had FannieBelle lead three of our loudest songs, and we almost raised the roof. After we'd finished Halsey came in looking rather funny, and told us that Hiiteni had passed away during Sivad. He said that the last thing she said was to keep things going, just as they were, and he said that he didn't want anyone to be unhappy over it. By that time we were all crying terribly, and he was choking himself, but he smiled and told us that he wanted things gayer and more cheerful than ever. He said that's the way Hiiteni would like us to be. Then he left, and Peggy Smith, who adored Hiiteni, asked us not to be unhappy at all – she herself was smiling – and then she asked Rastus to read the camp song to Hiiteni:

There's one to whom
We'll always pledge devotion,
One to whom
We'll always be true
She paved the way to Work, Health, Love Wohelo.[29]

Hiiteni, we will always love you. Everyone tried to sing, but it was the hardest thing I've ever had to do, so you can imagine what it meant for some of the old girls. We were all sobbing between every word, but we sang it thru twice. Then Peggy had us sing our loudest song: "Comrades" – then we went into dinner, and there we all laughed and talked. Maybe a little louder and more strained than usual, but everyone tried to act happy. The old Heavenlies called on Babs for her speech, and also made fools of several other girls – For instance, they made Dotty Wilson sing a cheer to herself, and they asked "Brooksie," one of the thinnest girls here, to speak three minutes on reducing.

After rest hour, the girls took the regular Sat. afternoon hike into South Casco. I stayed here with one or two other girls tho, and Bob McCurdy read to us.

What I think is about the most outstanding thing that Peggy and Halsey had us do is this – After dinner, they got a small band to-gether, and they asked us to dance. Now can you sort of imagine just how wonderful the spirit – everything – is here? I wish you could visit Wohelo, if only for an hour. You'd love it.

More to-morrow

Best love

Emmy

On July 30, Emily wrote another letter to her parents:

Sunday (written early Monday morn.)

Dear Mother and Dad:

On the whole, this has been about my most serious day at camp – Not that we all went around on tiptoe with drooping heads, but there was a certain quietness and a solemnity about camp to-day that is not generally here. This was probably or rather <u>was</u> caused by the fact that services for Hiiteni were held this afternoon. We spent the morning fixing up and cleaning up the tents and units. We also got flowers for Sivad and for Hiiteni's shack, so that when the people – loads of Hiiteni's friends came – arrived, Hiiteni's shack was just one mass of flowers. It was simply gorgeous. Besides the guests, and us, both Little Wohelo and Timanous came for the services, which were – beautiful. I can't say any more. They were very simple. An old friend of Hiiteni and Timanous spoke a little on the life and achievements of the Gulick's, and said wonderful things about them both – which were absolutely true. Phil [Phyllis] Radford, who has been at Wohelo almost ever since it started, was the only other person to make an address. She spoke on the ideals of Hiiteni, and also the things Hiiteni stood for. She also spoke a little about the spirit of Wohelo, and I don't think that she was <u>at all</u> wrong in saying that Hiiteni's spirit is the spirit of Wohelo, and that tho Hiiteni is gone, her spirit will always be here. I'm afraid this may sound gushy on paper, but if you had been here and heard it, if you knew what Wohelo was, if you had known Hiiteni, you'd know how true it is.

When Phil had finished speaking, Peggy Smith led: "There's One to Whom," and loads of the girls cried. One or two more songs were given – among them was one, the first verse of which was sung by Timanous, while we sang the second one. It's called "Old Chief Timanous," and is a lovely song.[30]

After services, the Timanous boys filed out. Then we left by way of Boulder road and started for Jordan Bay [Jordan Bay is the body of water enclosed by Raymond Cape and Frye's Island, the largest island in the lake, near the end of the cape]. I was heading for the Boulder Road with E.J. Wood, when I met one of the Timanous councilors who was also bound for the same place. It happened that I'd met him that nite the sisters were at Timanous so I asked him if he'd tell Bud about the ranch for me. I wasn't sure whether he knew or not. But Ed, the councilor, said that not only Bud but all of Timanous knew that we were going out West. He said that that's all Bud spoke of, so I guess the "kid" is pretty excited. Sort of sounds like it, doesn't it?

We had dinner at Jordon Bay, and walked back in the moonlight – which was gorgeous. (Jordan Bay is only a mile and a half away, so I didn't disobey orders.)

I haven't written Aunt Jane [Felix-Sophian] to thank her for the candy for the simple reason that I don't know her address.

I'm going to write the girls another special c/o Uncle Lou, this morning. Don't say I'm not doing right by any relatives – Whoopee!

More to-morrow

Best Love

Emmy

On July 30, Emily wrote the second letter of the day to her parents:

Monday

Mother and Dad dearest:

I'm awfully sorry you were worried about my having been sick.

If I had thought you would be I never would have mentioned anything about it. All it was was a head ache and stomach ache, and temperature. Lots of the girls had the same thing so it's all right. I ran a littler higher temperature than most of them, but I'm fine now – honest!

I got the dollar bill this morning. Thanks ever so much for it. It came just in time to take the place of one I'd just spent on stamps. Really, that's where most of my money is going – S'terrible – Whoopee!

Kay sent me a can of candy. I think it was lovely of her, and since it was only small, hard candy, I took a handful before I turned it in. You see, I got gyped on that taffy. I only got the one piece I took when the candy came. It's awfully hard to have to give it up – Lots of girls just keep it, but I've had enough will power (or whatever one needs) not to do that.

I wrote Mère Emmanuel [Notre Dame de Sion] a letter to-day in answer to one I received from her last week. You see, I wrote Notre Mère about two and a half weeks ago, and Mère Emmanuel answered it for her, altho Notre Mère tacked a darling note on the end of the letter. I'm going to write Mère Lodois to-morrow and I just finished a "special" to Polly and Flo. They should get it to-morrow. My how stamps do fly! I think I'm beginning to appreciate the value of money even tho mine has just slipped thru my fingers this summer. It's so nice tho to have it when you want something just awfully badly. You know what I mean – Remember Grant's in Petoskey [Michigan], when you saw some of the stuff I came home with. You were weak too, you know, even tho your weakness tended toward art, while mine – well, wait and see.

I went to pottery this afternoon and finished something for Dad. I also made good headway on something for Mother. The things I'm making aren't masterpieces by any means but there, it's just the idea of the thing – You understand, don't you.

All Timanous came over for council fire to-nite and I got to see and speak to Bud. Gee it was nice. I've missed him an awful lot, so you can imagine how much I've wanted both of you. Council fire was very nice, but Halsey wasn't there and it just wasn't the same without him, altho Peggy S. is a peach.

I wish you could meet her and all the girls – Especially FannieBelle (who I'm just nutty about), Dorrie Benson, and Peggy Wade. I don't know which I really like best – I have to run now – so

Bestest love
Emmy

On July 31, Emily wrote:

Tuesday
Dear Mother and Dad:

We changed to daylight saving time to-day, and therefore, have to go to bed while it's still light. That makes two things I don't like about camp – Daylight saving and the mosquitoes. Tough, isn't it?

The "gypsies" left on the trip around the lake trip this morning, but outside of that nothing happened. I took some pictures of the girls just before lunch, and have incidently used up all my films but two. I have some pretty good pictures tho. I had one taken of myself and it is being developed now. I'll send it to you if it turns out any good – If you want it.

Because we lost an hour's sleep last night on account of change of time, we had an extra long rest hour – I slept over two hours – Woof! Wonder how I'll get along without rest hour at home. I'm really getting into good habits here, and will come home "a changed girl." Really tho, I think camp is doing me just loads of good – at least I hope it is.

When are you leaving for the ranch? And could I bring a guest up there with me? I don't know whether I want to or not, but could I if I did? We haven't got more than about three and a half more weeks of camp. Isn't that awful! Anxious as I am to see you again, I just <u>hate</u> to think that camp is so nearly over – <u>I love it so</u>. Anna [Nichols] told me to tell you that she and her dad and the rest of them would put Bud and I on the train in Chicago, if you want. I think that was awfully nice of her, don't you? What should I tell her? Is it still so hot in K.C.? I sure hope not. Please take care of yourselves and leave as soon as you can.

Bestest love
Emmy

P.S. I think this will amuse you. I got a letter from "Mita" Lieberman the other day in which she said that "Skinny" said for her to tell me that he wasn't going to write me till I sent him a picture of me. Isn't that riotous! No Mother, I wasn't quite stupid enough to send one, and the poor boob can go hang – and

that's that. (Incidently there are some of the nicest councilors at Timanous.)
More love
(I'm not entirely "nuts" yet.)
Emmy

Emily's next letter to her parents on August 1, 1928 covered two days of experiences:

Wednesday (Thurs. Morn)
Dear Mother and Dad:
I went to jewelry this morning, and don't think I ever before realized <u>quite</u> how clumsy I am. Just wait till you see the things I've made you – <u>Just wait</u> Whoopee! It's been lots of fun making them tho, and I hope you'll like them.
Nothing was scheduled for this afternoon, but our unit was to go to Jordan Bay for dinner and ride back (horseback) in the moonlight. Frannie wasn't going to let me ride, so that I really didn't mind much when we didn't go. But anyhow, won't you write and say it's alright for me to do everything <u>please</u>. I feel fine.
We went for a tow after dinner this evening, and didn't come home till almost ten. Gee were we thrilled at staying up that late. You don't realize what late hours mean up here!
I have to rush now for swimming, but I'll write you a longer letter to-morrow.
Best love ever
Emmy

On August 2, 1928, Estelle wrote the following letter to Emily:

Thursday
Dearest Emmy
I shall be very glad for you to have the book of poems you want but by the time I find out how much money to send to the publishing house it will be too late for you to receive it at camp – so I believe it will be a better idea for you to send for it while we are at the ranch which is just a short distance from Seattle. I will enquire at the Bookman and other places here in the meantime. Perhaps I may be able to find it here. In that event I shall send it right on to you.

What did the Heavenlies do to you, as a punishment for being a newcomer? I made up my mind a long time ago that you chose wisely in going to Wohelo and am very happy indeed that you are so also lately devoted to it. I was very much impressed with your description of the events following the passing of Hiiteni.

To-day has been another scorching day – We are taking Mrs. Julius Lyons to dinner this evening – I nearly sweltered at a luncheon Mrs. Lightner gave at her studio today. [Rest of letter lost]

On August 2, 1928, Emily wrote the following letter to her parents:

Thursday (Friday Morn.)
Dear Mother and Dad:
I went to pottery this morning, and finished another work of art. This was for Mother. The next, and last thing I make will be for both of you – (Not that the others aren't also, but – You understand.)

We tried to elect our crew captain last night. It was between Peggy Wade and Babs Van Duyn – it was terrible! No one knew which one to vote for – They're so evenly matched, and both such good sports. We voted twice and it was a tie both times. So Babs took crew out this morning, and Peggy took it out right after rest hour. Well, I've never seen such a startling, almost perfect crew in my life as when Peggy took it out. The other girls seemed to think the same as I did, because Peggy was elected by a large majority. I'm awfully glad, but it would have been just as well if Babs had gotten it.

Heavenlies left for an overnight trip on the houseboat at about four o'clock – Gee I had fun! We made string bracelets, danced, had a marshmallow fight and everything – I loved it.

I'm enclosing a picture – It's not very good but I hope you like it.

Bestest love
Emmy

Emily's next letter to her parents was dated August 3, 1928:

Friday (Sat. Morn.)
Dear Mother and Dad:
We got back from the houseboat trip this morning, so we

consequently spent the time fixing up the tent. At lunch it was announced that Boulders would go on the houseboat this evening, that Barracks would spend the evening (or rather the nite) at Wohelo Island, and that Lewa would go for a moonlight ride. That left Heavenlies and Haeremai without anything to do, so Frannie Cooper invited Haeremai to a Baby Party to be given by Heavenlies in the evening. After rest hour we had a short unit meeting and decided on what games to play. Frannie also appointed a supper comittee. Then the councilors went to South Casco to buy the "prizes," and the rest of us proceeded to jewelry. At five a bugle blew for dip, and after that we came back to our tents and got up our costumes. You should have seen some of them – they were riots! I wore my silk pajamas, and rolled the legs way up above my knees. Then I put a black belt around my middle, and behold me in a pair of glorified rompers. I also wore a pair of silk stockings as socks and my city shoes. On my head I had a great big black bow – Wow! What a sight!

The party was a huge success. We had party hats, and we played drop the handkerchief, "pin the beak on a heavenly bird," farmer in the dell, London Bridge, and many other very entertaining games. Toward the end, we danced. It was <u>loads</u> of fun. More to-morrow!

Best love ever

Emmy

P.S. I'm <u>awfully</u> glad it's cooler in K.C.

Emily's August 4 letter said:

Saturday

Dear Mother and Dad:

Rode into South Casco on the truck this afternoon, and came back to camp almost broke. I don't know what's wrong with my stockings, but they either disappear or else get torn beyond the mending stage. So that when I went into South Casco all the stockings I possessed were the ones on my legs – and those were borrowed! How's that!

I consequently purchased six pairs at 25 [cents] per pair. I then got myself a bathing cap, a knife (I lost mine, and I just had to have one) –, some moccasins (my tennis shoes are worn out), and some ice cream. That leaves me a little over a dollar – but I won't need any more until I'm ready to leave camp. Incidently, camp breaks up two weeks from this coming Friday, and Bud and I will arrive in Chicago at 4.30 P.M. on August 5 [*sic*, should be August 25]. I sure will be sorry when camp's over.

This evening we went over to a Little Wohelo council fire. It was awfully cute, and they had a darling marionette show afterward. You would have loved it –

When do you leave for the ranch? I hope you have a wonderful trip out there.

Loads and loads of love

Emmy

Estelle wrote the following to Emily around August 4, 1928:

Dearest Emmy:

This morning I received your Wednesday letter, written Thursday morning and mailed on Friday – There is one thing I'd like you to learn, that is: the value of <u>time</u> –

Dad and I do not believe it would be a good idea for you to bring a guest on this trip to the ranch. Next time perhaps – I'll give you my reasons when we meet –

Mr. Nathan of the "Bookman" promised me to try to find the "Magic Ring" for you –

Why it will be splendid if Anna and her family can put you on the train in Chicago – I think it was fine for her to think of it.

Mrs. Schoenberg is leaving this evening for the East. After spending a week in Atlantic City, she will visit Hiawatha. She told me she was planning to see you at your camp – if you will have at least one visitor. Did you ever hear anything further from your cousin Lawrence?

[Illegible] called up on the telephone to-day asking for you. His sister Ruth has become engaged to a young man in Youngstown, Ohio. He, Lee, came home for the weekend in honor of the event – He says he works from 7.45 A. M. to 5.30 P.M., so has not had time to write to the gang. He took your address, however, so now you have something to live for –

I called up Daddy at the office to be sure to write you giving you permission to indulge in camp activities. He said he wrote you last week telling you to use your discretion. You must have the letter by now –

Much love

Mother

Emily's August 5, 1928 letter said

Sunday (Monday Morn.)
Dear Mother and Dad:
We fixed up our tent all nice and neat this morning and started the week right – It won't last long tho, I'm afraid. We had the usual long Sunday Sivad – There were a lot of guests. Little Wohelo was there too, and Halsey blushed scarlet when Little Wohelo sang a very complimentary cheer to him and we joined in. It was more fun.

After rest hour, I began a green and white string necklace for FannieBelle which took me all afternoon. They're very fascinating to make. I'll show you how when I get home.

After dinner I went down to Barracks with Anna, Babs Eastman, Babs Stearns, Muggins Smith, and Hildegarde Hathaway. I stayed there and ate fruit with them till Taps.

I'm going to start working for water baby this week and hope to get it by a week from Monday (to-day). Incidently, I rowed an island, and passed two dives and breast stroke for it this morning – how's that!

Best love
Emmy
P.S. I'm going to be <u>terribly</u> busy this week so my letters will be <u>very</u> brief.

Emily's August 6 letter read:

Monday (Tues. Morn.)
Dear Mother and Dad:
In the letter I wrote this morning (Monday), I told you that I was going to try for water baby and that I'd passed some things in the morning. This afternoon I rowed another island. I'll get there yet. This (Tuesday) morning I paddled an island, passed my canoe test, and my back stroke. I expect to row another island (maybe two) this afternoon, and I'm going to try to pass some more stuff. Whee!

Council fire to-nite wasn't very good – It wasn't serious enough – everyone kept laughing. The odds and ends had the count. They began it with a very clever marionette show, but the rest was silly. Only the Timanous councilors came, so I didn't get to see Bud. I imagine the brothers will be over here for dinner some time this week tho – Here's hoping anyhow.

I'm sorry it's so hot in K.C. At present, I'm just shivering – from my dip maybe, but the weather is <u>pretty</u> cold.

More to-morrow

Best love

Emmy

Around August 7, 1928, all letters that Emily wrote to her parents in Kansas City were automatically forwarded by the post office in Kansas City to c/o Joseph F. Reed of Marble, Washington, as Estelle and Abraham already had left for Washington by car.

Emily's August 7, 1928 letter read:

Tuesday (Wednesday Morn.)

Dear Mother and Dad:

I spent the afternoon to-day passing things for water baby. I expect to be finished Thursday at the latest – you see, I passed side stroke this (Wed.) morning, so that all I have left to do is my row boat test and two islands to row. Yea! I'm so glad.

This evening Heavenlies cooked out over at Rookies [Island]. Some of the girls, including Mac Frothingham and Sue Miller, spent the night there. That left Peggy Wade and I all alone in the tent, and we talked till awfully late. But late as we were up, we could still hear the girls over at the island making noise after we both went to bed. They had a marvelous time.

The money you sent came just at the right time, Mother. I wanted to buy a beautifully bound book of peachy poetry called "The Magic Casement" [fairy poetry collection assembled by Alfred Noyes, published 1909], and I didn't have enough money, but now that your dollar came I have forty two cents left – Whoopee!

Thanks loads for the cards. I certainly appreciate your sending them to me, and I'm awfully glad to have them.

By the way, do you want me to address my letters to the ranch beginning with the eleventh? And if so, what is the address? I'm dreading the thought of camp ending, but I'm looking forward to going out West and can hardly wait till I see you again. Be sure to take care of yourselves, and I hope you have a wonderful trip –

Loads of love

Emmy

The distance between South Casco, Maine and Spokane, Washington is about 3,000 miles. Some of the poems included in Alfred Noyes' *The Magic Casement* were:

I Know a Bank by William Shakespeare
Where the Bee Sucks by William Shakespeare
Nurslings of Immortality by Percy Bysshe Shelley
Puck's Song by Rudyard Kipling
On a Midsummer-Night by William Shakespeare
A Holyday Night by John Milton
Falstaff and the Fairies by William Shakespeare
The Bugles of Dreamland by Fiona Macleod
The Dream-Fair by Alfred Noyes
The Horns of Elfland by Alfred, Lord Tennyson

Emily's August 8 1928 letter to her parents said:

Wednesday
Dear Mother and Dad:
    I didn't get a letter to-day in either mail, and I missed hearing from you. How is everything? Has the heat let up yet? It's been awfully cold here during the past week – we've worn our jerseys and our heavy sweaters both.
    I was going to row a couple of islands this afternoon, but I slept so late that I barely got to supper in time – Woof!
    Nothing happened this evening. I went in Senhalone alone, Hiiteni's shack, with Fritz Laundon. We stayed there for awhile and read. Frannie was going to read poetry in Heavenly circle, and there was dancing on the tennis court, so I divided my time between the two places. It was fun. Dorrie wasn't feeling well, so I spent some time in her tent rubbing her back. This has been one of the quietest days in almost two weeks, so I'm afraid there isn't much to say. I'll try and write a longer one to-morrow.
    Bestest love
    Emmy

On August 9, Emily wrote:

Thursday
Dear Mother and Dad:
    After all, do you think it's quite fair to say anything about

when I write and mail my letter to you, because you know how much is always happening here, and I can only write when I can snatch a minute – We have no regular letter writing time, and I'm the <u>only</u> girl in camp who writes home every day. Now – how's that!

It seems so funny to be writing you out to the ranch. I hope you enjoyed the trip, and I'm sure you'll have a wonderful time now that you're there. That last wish was mostly for Mother – I know how much she loves it.

I haven't heard anything more from Lawrence. That breaks me all up, of course, but I would like to see him. I'll be glad to see Mrs. Schoenberg if she gets here before camp is over – but I somehow doubt if she will – here's hoping tho.

I spent this morning on the dock. There were tryouts for the relays for Water Sports day – which is to be Tuesday. All I tried out for was side stroke, and that wore me out – besides, I wasn't half fast enough, so I doubt if I shall be in anything much. I don't really mind tho, and shall enjoy watching it just as much as if I were taking part in it.

I rowed my two islands this afternoon and almost passed out it was so hot. Gee the weather is changeable up here.

I played tennis for awhile after dinner this evening, then I watched Halsey and Mary Lois Paschal (an awfully attractive councilor) – play – Gee they're good!

More to-morrow

Bestest ever

Emmy

P.S. Anna wants to be remembered to you.

On August 10, 1928, Emily addressed her letter to her parents as follows: "Dr. and Mrs. A. Sophian, c/o Upper Columbia Orchards, Marble, Washington." Her remaining letters to her parents carried this address. Her August 10, 1928 letter said:

Friday

Dear Mother and Dad:

I started to play tennis with Mac Frothingham this morning, but some girls wanted to play off a tournament so we let them have the court. I stayed and refereed and got them all mixed up – but they didn't mind and I had fun.

Our unit had riding this afternoon, and I finally talked Frannie into letting me try it again. Gee it was fun! I think I rode better than I ever have before, but I don't think I'll go any more this summer.

Say, I haven't gotten more than two letters from you this week – and I miss hearing from you – I guess it's because of the trip tho. I sure hope you enjoy yourselves at the ranch.

I'm sorry there's no more news, but I'll try to write more tomorrow.

Lots of love

Emmy

P.S. I'm sorry you don't think I look well in that picture. I've gained 8½ pounds and am a pound and half overweight! Oof!

On August 11, Emily wrote:

Saturday

Dear Mother and Dad:

We went thru Water Sports day program this morning and I never was so thrilled in my life – Heavenlies just walked off with all the races and diving contests. It was wonderful! I sure wish you could both be here on Tuesday when the real program is going to take place. I know you'd enjoy it so much!

This afternoon I wanted to stay here and fool around, but I wanted to see Bud so I rode to South Casco in the Migis with a bunch of other girls. When I got there I found out that he had been made a Voyager at last council fire and was resting up from a trip the Voyagers had just taken. I'm so proud of him, but I was so disappointed because I didn't get to see him.

Nothing much happened this evening altho there was dancing on the tennis court. How do you like the ranch? Please write me all about everything.

Lots and lots of love

Emmy

On August 11, 1928, Estelle sent a post card to Emily. On its front side was a color photo of the Public Library of Kearney, Nebraska. The postcard read:

I shall miss your letters all along the route but expect a great many when we arrive in Marble. I shall write a long letter my first opportunity. This is our first day out [on their trip from Kansas City to Marble, Washington].

Love Mother

Meanwhile, Emily faithfully sent a letter to her parents for August 12, 1928:

Sunday
Dear Mother and Dad:
We had Sivad on the houseboat this morning while we crossed the lake to Douglass Hill [at 1,400 feet above sea level and 1145 feet above the surface of Sebago Lake, it is the principal peak of the Saddleback Mountains]. I don't know why they chose to-day, but anyhow, we climbed to the top of the mountain. I rode part of the way in the truck, but had to walk quite a way. The blueberries were marvelous, and I've never seen such a marvelous view as from the top of the mountain – We could see the ocean way in the distance and also Portland slightly. There were mountain peaks all around us [Peaked and Tiger Mountains], and we could see fourteen or fifteen lakes [and ponds, including Sabbathday, Perley's, Fitch's, Southeast, Tobacco or Hancock, Peabody, and Great Hancock[31]] besides all of Lake Sebago, which is no lily pond. It was really wonderful, but I ate so much and was so tired that I was a wreck by the time we reached camp again. But then, everyone else was worn out too, so that's all right.

I hope you love the ranch, and can hardly wait till I can join you there, tho the thought of leaving camp half kills me.

Please write me all about everything, tho I don't imagine I'll be able to get many more letters from you.

Lots and lots of love
Emmy

Emily's August 13 letter read:

Monday
Dear Mother and Dad:
Heavenlies had the "count" for council fire to-nite and so we spent almost the whole day rehearsing for it. In case I haven't told you about it, the count comes at the end of council fire, and is given by a different unit each week. It consists of a group of

songs, dances, short sketches, etc. pertaining to the outstanding events that have occurred during the week. Some of them have been awfully clever, but personally, I think the Heavenlies count takes the cake – and so do most of the other girls. Gee it was just darling. The songs weren't particularly well sung, but they were so peppy that everybody liked them – and we had loads of fun doing everything.

To-morrow is Water Sports day, so I have to turn in now.
Bestest love
Emmy

On August 14, Emily wrote:

Tuesday
Dear Mother and Dad:
This has been one of the most marvelous days I've ever spent. Gee it was great! You have no idea what you missed by not being here for Water Sports Day – here's a sort of program of the day – with results.

At 10.15 a bugle blew and we all met on the tennis court. When everybody was there, we marched around the court twice singing "Camp Wohelo girls are we," then we marched down Boulder Hill, still singing, and around Boulder dock. We then lined up in three rows along the shore and gave a cheer first to the guests, next to Highland Nature Camp, which came to watch us, then to Little Wohelo, and last to Timanous. The whole camp was on top of the houseboat, which was anchored about 35 yds. out from the dock.

The first event was the umbrella race. A girl from every unit dove in with a closed umbrella, swam to the float twenty five yds. away, opened the umbrella, and swam back. "Ginger" Condict represented Heavenlies and won easily for us. That gave us five points.

The next event was the undressing race. A girl from every unit dove off the float with her clothes on, took them off as fast as she could, then swam to the dock. Peggy Wade raced for Heavenlies and won for us – giving us five more points.

Next came the unit diving. All that consisted of was a dive by every girl in every unit to show the parents that there wasn't a girl in camp who couldn't go off the spring board. Every unit got 100%. Isn't that marvelous!

Next came some exhibition life saving. Ruth Price broke strangle holds on Bob Hertzler, then "life saved" him to the dock. A few minutes after that, Bob McCurdy, all dressed up in city clothes, jumped off a dock and pretended that she was drowning. Sue Miller swam out and "life saved" her. It was really awfully effective.

The next event was an inter-unit relay. It sounds sort of complicated, but it really wasn't – this is how it worked. A girl from every unit dove from the dock and swam over to the float breast stroke. As soon as she touched it, the H.C. from her unit touched the next girl and she swam back sidestroke. When she reached the dock, the team's captain touched the next girl and she swam to the float using single overarm. When she got there, the H.C. touched off the next one who swam back using any stroke she wanted to. The "free styles" were followed by another girl doing the breast stroke – and the whole thing was gone thru again – by different girls of course. Sue Miller really won this for Heavenlies, tho some of the others did pretty well. Anyhow, Heavenlies won the relay and ten more points.

Next comes the squad swimming which I can't explain – but which is marvelous. I have some good pictures of it that I'll show you week after next.

The last thing on the morning program was the form diving – the best divers in camp doing different kinds of dives. Some were marvelous. There were three girls from Lewa, three from Haeremai, three from Boulders, three from Barracks, and <u>seven</u> from Heavenlies. Hows that! It was individual competition tho, not for unit points, tho of course every unit wanted its own divers to win first, second, and third places.

As it was Heavenlies won the first two places – Sue Miller came in first by a large majority, and Babs Van Duyn came in second. I forgot to mention tho that while the judges were adding up the marks for the different dives, Halsey did some gorgeous ones from the tower, and finally made a perfect dive off Heavenly Rock. It was simply beautiful, because the Rock is over twice as high as the diving tower – and the tower is <u>no</u> footstool.

The afternoon events began at three o'clock with a formal tow. After this was aquaplaning – Some of the gals did marvelous stunts on the board. After the aquaplaning came a procession of five row boats, one from each unit, with an H.C. and a senior councilor in each one. The row boats had been decorated up very cleverly. Five points went to Barracks for winning first as the most original one. Heavenlies came in second and got three points. Gee it was clever! Frannie and Jenny had put a flat raft across the rowboat and had strung a clothes line from the front to the back. They had the wildest socks, pajamas, sweaters, etc. hanging from the line I've ever seen. They had lots of junk lying around in the middle of the raft, and Frannie was sitting in the back on a legless chair. She had a pipe in her mouth, a yachting cap on her head and wore sailor pants and some kind of sweater. Jenny had on a black bathing suit and wore black stockings on her legs, arms, and head – having holes cut out for her eyes and mouth. On the middle of the clothes line they had a sign pinned: Robinson Crusoe and his Man Friday – Gee it was cute!

This procession was followed by a row boat race as soon as the decorations were taken off them. The H.C.'s and Senior councilors who had been in them in the procession, raced them. Frannie was doing fine when somehow, she gave a hard pull and missed the water almost entirely. She fell back in the boat and hurt herself pretty badly, I'm afraid. Of course, Heavenlies "didn't come in." The war canoe drill was next – It was perfect and then there was exhibition of how to upset, rescue, and right a sailing canoe.

The last thing on the program was the war canoe race – It is the event of the day. Nothing else counts much. Well, Heavenlies won! And by almost a half a boat's length too – Whee! Gee it was glorious! I've never heard such screaming and shouting! We carried Peggy Wade all around the dock on our shoulders. Then we came up to the unit and dressed. We also stuck blue ribbons all over us, then started to yell some more. When everyone was ready, we marched over to the tennis court and paraded around it carrying Peg on our shoulders and singing "Here's to Heavenlies." Gee it was fun! Then we took our place in the middle of the tennis court and had a real feast, while the rest of the units ate their regular dinner in the four corners of the court!

Wasn't it a marvelous day?

Lots of love

Emmy

P.S. Heavenlies also won the day. We had 33 points. Boulders, which was our closest rival, had 14 – Whoops!

On August 15, Emily continued:

Wednesday

Dear Mother and Dad:

There was Water Sports Day at little camp this morning and Fritz and I were going over in a canoe, but it was so hot on the lake that we stayed here. Gee it was just sweltering all day to-day – In fact, it was so hot that none of us had the energy to do anything except lie around all afternoon. We spent a lot of time in the water too tho, of course.

The unit that won the chart competition left on the houseboat for an aquaplaning trip – lucky bums. We had ice cream for supper tho, and had a dip just before taps so it wasn't so hard on us left at camp after all.

I've gotten your postcards, and am glad you are having such a lovely time.

Lot of love

Emmy

On August 16, Emily went on:

Thursday

Dear Mother and Dad:

Went to jewelry this morning and really accomplished a lot. I almost finished something that I've been having a lot of trouble with. You see, small things are hard for me cause I'm so terribly clumsy with my hands.

This afternoon was another sweltering one. I fooled around for awhile, then went down to Senhalone with Jannie Smith. We stayed there and looked at books and pictures till way after second [word?] had blown. It was more fun. We found some awfully cute pictures of Halsey when he was a little boy, and some of Hiiteni's scrap books were most interesting.

There was nothing scheduled this evening, so I just fooled around and talked with Adelaide Greene and Mac. Jannie was there too, and we all came over to the tennis court later and danced.

More to-morrow. Hope you're having a good time.

Heaps of love

Emmy

P.S. My "Magic Casements" came in this evening mail and I love it. I like the poems in "The Magic Ring" even better tho, so I hope you can get it for me. More love - Emmy

On August 16, 1928, Estelle wrote to Emily and Bud a long letter from Spokane, Washington on Davenport Hotel stationary. She addressed the letter to "Miss Emily Sophian, c/o Luther Gulick Camp, South Casco, Maine." The letter read as follows:

Thursday
Dearest Emmy and Buddy:

We arrived in Spokane this morning after a fine trip. We are now in Colville where Mr. Reed met us and will take us to the ranch – I have tried to write on the way but it has been impossible.

Some few days ago, I sent to Halsey your tickets – a full fare for Emmy and half fare for Buddy – also a check for seventy-five dollars which he will cash and give to you. I sent that much in case there is a question about Buddy's fare. You will then have sufficient money. Of course I expect both of you to be careful about the amount of money you spend. Remember what I told you that it is vulgar for children to spend money extravagantly. On the train the food portions are very large – one portion is plenty for two and you should order your meals accordingly – and whatever you do, please do not fuss. That would not reflect credit on your family.

Anna will not be able to put you on the train because you go out at different depots and her family will not be in Chicago. An agent of the Burlington R.R. will meet you as you arrive in Chicago and take you to the Union Station from which place your train for the West departs. You can have your dinner there if you can wait that long. Dr. Pickard will write to a Miss Polly at the Bookshop to look out for you and I know you will be sufficiently entertained among the books until it is time to get on your train which leaves at 11.30 but can get on at about 10 o'clock – Do not for any reason leave the train at the different stops. If you want anything, send the porter out for it. This is very important and Daddy and I particularly make this request to which I know you will comply.

I hope you, Emmy received the sweater, blouses and skirt I sent by parcels post the day before we left Kansas City.

You can check your trunk (using both tickets – the one from Portland to Chicago and the one from Chicago to Spokane) direct to Spokane. I explained this in my letter to Halsey so that you will not have to be bothered rechecking in Chicago as I wrote in my other letter.

There will be a piece of your ticket left over Emmy, the part from Chicago to Kansas City. Do not lose this or destroy it as we can cash it in – Or better still you can give it to Anna to give to her father who said he can use it and will then refund to us –

Be sure to put your raincoat into your trunk because you will need it on the trip home – It would ruin your good coat to use it in the car as the roads are very dusty –

Both of you please send all your bedding things you will not use on the ranch, in your duffle bags by parcels post to Kansas City.

Emmy please try to send your trunk a day or two before you leave so that it will be in Spokane when you arrive as it is too far to send back for it after we once leave for the ranch.

Buddy, be sure to bring your riding breeches and wool hose with you.

After you read this letter Emmy, either mail it to Bud or send it to him by Halsey –

Be sure to look for the Burlington man as you get off the train in Chicago – It is a long distance from the Michigan [Street] Central Station to the Union Station and this man will see that you get over there. Dr. Pickard … [rest of letter lost]

On August 17, 1928, Emily wrote:

Friday
Dear Mother and Dad:
Went to jewelry this morning and wanted to make a ring for mother. I had a peachy stone picked out and a darling ring all planned – this Floydie told me I wouldn't have time to make a third piece – Gee I was disappointed. So I just stayed and fooled around all morning.

This afternoon we went over to Timanous for the annual circus. I had more fun – all those <u>little boys</u> were so cute. Tumbling was the first thing on the program. The boys really did quite well, and Bud was awfully cute, but "Brother" Lewis, a boy about fourteen, was simply marvelous. He did everything the others did – only better; then when the regular tumbling was over he and Sonny Gaston, a councilor, came out and did some very good stunts. There were one or two more things, then as the last tumbling act, two of the councilors came out, stood in the middle of the mat holding a fairly large hoop with paper wound around it. Then they set fire to the paper and "Brother" came out and turned a summersault thru the burning hoop – He wasn't even singed. Isn't that great!

The next event on the program was some exhibition horseback riding. Bud sure sits a horse well. He did himself proud in the Roman riding when he came in with one foot on the white horse, one foot on the other. I was awfully proud of him.

The last thing on the program was a minstrel show. It was very cleverly done, and Mit was a scream. Bob Hertzler's brother did some "magician" tricks that none of us could catch on to, and Bob was so proud of him I thought he'd pop.

When the program was over, we went to the different booths and tried to win candy. I spent quite some time on one booth where we had to throw baseballs and knock down some dummies. I didn't have much luck and I wanted some candy, so "Brother" knocked down two of the dummies, and gave me the candy. I shared it with him, so from then on we formed a partnership and went from booth to booth to-gether. It was loads of fun, because whenever we didn't win anything, "Brother" went and helped himself to the candy anyhow. Bud brought me everything he won too, so that by the time the truck came to take us home, I had quite a fill of candy. In spite of the fact tho, they gave me two huge handfuls to take back to camp with me, and pelted the truck with marshmallows till we drove off. Gee it was fun.

How do you like the ranch? I hope you're having a marvelous time. Write and tell me about it won't you?

Lots of love
Emmy

On August 18, Emily wrote:

Saturday (Sun. Morn.)
Dear Mother and Dad:
Went to jewelry again this morning and looked around. I had a pretty good time and there wasn't much else to do because it rained cats and dogs. Whoops!

I rode into South Casco on the truck this afternoon, and got there just as Bud was leaving. I got to speak to him tho – Whee! He had ridden in on horseback in the rain and was having a wonderful time – Wouldn't he tho! Gee he's cute. I'm just nuts about him, so I guess the separation is doing us good. When we got back to camp Fritz and I went to jewelry again, and made Bud a narrow hammered bracelet out of some copper scraps – It was fun.

We thought Heavenly Initiation was going to be to-nite, so there was a great deal of excitement in Heavenlies to-nite. It was a lot of fun – but nothing happened.

Please don't mind if you don't get many more letters, but this being the last week of camp I'm afraid things are going to be happening pretty fast. I'll try to write something ever day tho – but don't worry if I don't.

Heaps of love
Emmy
P.S. How's the ranch? Do you ride, Mother?

On August 19, Emily wrote:

Sunday
Dear Mother and Dad:
We had an extra long Sivad this morning since this is our last Sunday here. After that we only had a short time till lunch, but I went over to the tennis court and watched a tournament. We had a marvelous lunch – chicken, rice, ice cream and everything. Whoopee!

I spent my afternoon in a very elevating way – I'm quite proud of myself. I wrote letters and copied poetry. I got some peachy ones too. My Magic Casements is here – as I think I've already told you – and I just adore the poems in it.

Bob McCurdy read to us after supper to-nite. It's an awfully cute book, "The Laughingest Lady," but I doubt she'll finish before we leave.

I hope you're having a wonderful time –
Lots of love
Emmy
P.S. This is an awfully "blah" letter and I'm sorry – but everybody's talking and I can't think –

On Monday, August 20, 1928, Sister Lodois of Sion wrote a postcard to Emily. On the front of the card is a color photo of the Medici Fountain (Luxembourg's Garden).[32] Sister Lodois placed the card in an envelope with a return address of Notre Dame de Sion, 3823 Locust Street, Kansas City, Missouri. On her card, Sister Lodois wrote that Notre Mère asked to be remembered to Emily. Sister Lodois also asked Emily never to forget Sion during her travels to many places during vacations. Sister Lodois' card to Emily first traveled to South Casco, Maine (which Emily had already left), then was forwarded to Marble, Washington (which Emily had already left), and finally reached her at home in Georgian Court in Kansas City.

On August 24, 1928, Emily wrote:

Friday
Dear Mother and Dad:
    I'm awfully sorry I didn't get to write this week, but things happened so fast that I didn't have a minute. I'm going to try to make up for it now tho, by writing you as complete an account of the week as I can. This letter probably won't reach you more than a day or two before I will, but – nevertheless –
    Tuesday – Timanous Water Sports Day happened this morning. It was pretty good, and Bud was awfully cute, but on the whole, it really can't compare with our Water Sports program – which was simply <u>marvelous</u>. I went to Timanous in Mrs. Wilson's car with Babs Lewis, Leo [Leonora] McClure, and Frannie Cooper. We got back to camp just as lunch was over, so they (Wayne and Emily [the camp cooks]) got us up a regular feast. Whoops!
    I went to jewelry this afternoon and made something for my kid brother. As I was going back, around five o'clock, I discovered that we were having a costume dance on the tennis court after dinner, and that the costumes were to be gotten up from the camp uniform – More fun! I finally got a bright idea tho. I got Babs, Mac, and Fritz to be the three musketeers, and I went as d'Artagnan. We wore our bloomers pulled way up, riding boots, riding socks, and riding shirts. We had red bandanas tied around our waists as sashes, and we wore our sailor hats cocked on one side with ferns pinned on to take the place of feathers. Gee it was fun, and everybody loved our costumes – Incidently I forgot to mention that we had very fetching gottees [goatees] and mustaches pained on. I wish you could have seen us.
    Wednesday – I packed all morning, and half an hour before lunch they had old campers rest hour. All the old girls spent rest in their last year's tent, and the new girls adjourned to the old riding circle.
    When Heavenlies returned to their unit after rest hour, all the old Heavenlies were waiting for us. They made us put our middies on backwards and braid our hair in twenty pigtails. The

girls with long hair had to wear it in a knot at least two inches high on the top of their heads. We went to lunch singing "Here's to Heavenlies, girls," and all the other units looked at us enviously. It was loads of fun.

I just fooled around this afternoon, being very busy, but not really doing anything.

Banquet was this evening, and it was just too perfect to be true. Every girl was given a big picture of Hiiteni, and the place cards were darling. I'll show you mine Tuesday. I can't describe Banquet – I'll try and tell you about it when I see you, tho.

Thursday – To-day wasn't what one might call a cheerful day. Everybody was going around getting addresses, promising to write, and then rushing up to the trunk house to put some forgotten article in her trunk. Our weaving, pottery and jewelry was given to us, too. I'll have only one piece of jewelry (that I myself made) to show you, because I gave or rather swapped bracelets with Dorrie. I have a stunning (at least I think so) ring too that Fritz made for me.

We had a last Sivad after dinner (which was incidently a corn roast) this evening, and I've never seen such a miserable bunch of girls in my life. We were all crying, sniffling, getting addresses, and crying some more. We sang too, but the songs were so weak that half the time we didn't even all know that one was being sung – Ooh!

I didn't get much sleep to-nite, 'cause we all gathered on Peggy's bed and talked till all hours of the nite.

Friday – As soon as reveille blew this morning we all jumped out of bed, ran into Heavenly circle, and cheered Frannie. Then the trouble began. Gee we hated to put on city clothes. I went to breakfast but couldn't eat a thing. By the time I got on the boat [steamboat] I was crying so hard I could hardly see anything – So was everyone. Gee I've just adored camp. This has been one of the marviest summers I've ever spent, and I just don't know how to thank you enough for sending me to Wohelo. Every minute has been perfect, but I can hardly wait till I see you Tuesday.

Loads and loads of love

Emmy

The letter above was Emily's last one to her parents during the summer of 1928.

Wohelo campers who achieved Water Baby by the end of the 1928 summer session were:

Suzanne Arguimbau
Lois Ashley
Muriel Behrens
Frances Bell
Doris Benson
Eleanor Bingham
Bettina Blanding
Catherine Bolster
Susan Brockett
Elizabeth Brooks
Betty Cluff
Nancy Cluff
Barbara Colbron
Julia Denison
Sally Drew
Deborah Ann Durstine
Ellen Eastman
Helen Feeney
Louisa Ford
Betty French
Janet French
Margaret Frothingham
Caroline Hales
Hildegarde Hathaway
Harriet Hilts
Mary Holmes
Eunice Jameson
Elizabeth Knowland
Frances Laundon
Edith Longsdorf
Virginia Macomber
Susan Merritt
Jean Palmer
Mary Lois Paschal
Frances Phillips
Margaret Price
Frieda Purdum
Eleanor Rogers
Eleanor Schreyer
Marguerite Smith
Nancy Smith

Wohelo campers hiking, circa 1928–1929. Image credit:
Wohelo Camp Archives, Raymond, Maine.

Charlotte Vetter Gulick in front of fireplace in her bungalow Senhalone, Wohelo, South Casco, Maine. Image credit: Wohelo Camp Archives, Raymond, Maine.

Halsey Gulick diving off Heavenlies Rocks, Wohelo, South Casco, Maine. Image credit: Wohelo Camp Archives, Raymond, Maine.

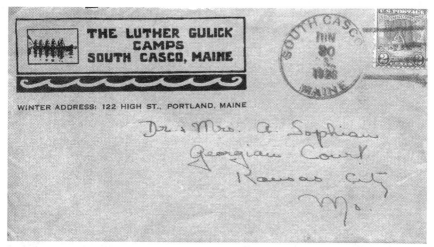

Envelop of Emily Sophian's letter to her parents, Dr. and Mrs. Sophian, on Wohelo stationary, June 30, 1928. Image credit: Sophian Archives, Fairway, Kansas.

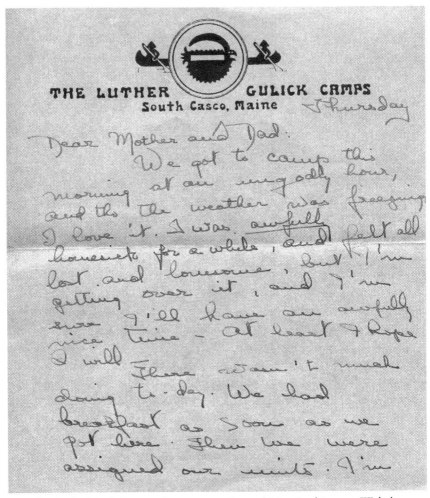

Emily Sophian's letter to her parents, Dr. and Mrs. Sophian, on Wohelo stationary, June 30, 1928. Image credit: Sophian Archives, Fairway, Kansas.

Estelle Sophian's letter to her daughter Emily, summer 1928.
Image credit: Sophian Archives, Fairway, Kansas.

Notre Mère Irene de Sion (right, head of convent and school) and Mère Emmanuel de Sion (later succeeded Notre Mère Irene as head of convent and school), Notre Dame de Sion, Kansas City, Missouri. Image credit: Notre Dame de Sion Archives, Kansas City, Missouri.

Envelop of letter to Emily Sophian at Wohelo camp in Maine, 1928, from Mère Emmanuel de Sion and Notre Mère Irene de Sion, Notre Dame de Sion, Kansas City, Missouri. Image credit: Sophian Archives, Fairway, Kansas.

First page of letter to Emily Sophian at Wohelo camp in Maine, from Mère Emmanuel de Sion and Notre Mère Irene de Sion, Notre Dame de Sion, Kansas City, Missouri. Image credit: Sophian Archives, Fairway, Kansas.

Envelop sent in August 1928 by Mère Lodois and Notre Mère Irene de Sion
(Notre Dame de Sion, Kansas City, Missouri) to Emily Sophian after she
had left Wohelo, South Casco, Maine. The envelop traveled from Maine to
Washington state, and finally back to Georgian Court, Kansas City, Missouri,
when Emily finally received it. Image credit: Sophian Archives, Fairway, Kansas.

Card inside envelop sent to Emily by Mère Lodois and Notre Mère Irene de Sion, Notre Dame de Sion, Kansas City, Missouri, August 1928. An image of the Medici Fountain is on the reverse side. Image credit: Sophian Archives, Fairway, Kansas.

Medici Fountain on the front side of card sent to Emily by Mère Lodois and Notre Mère Irene de Sion, Notre Dame de Sion, Kansas City, Missouri, in August 1928. Image credit: Sophian Archives, Fairway, Kansas.

Steamer on Sebago Lake boarding Wohelo campers at the end of a summer session to take them to Sebago Lake Railroad Station. Image credit: Wohelo Camp Archives, Raymond, Maine.

1920s Buick similar to the one driven by the Abraham Sophian family from Kansas City to Marble, Washington state and back in August–September 1928. Image credit: Sophian Archives, Fairway, Kansas.

Epilogue

On September 12, 1928, Emily began her junior year at the new campus of the French Institute of Notre Dame de Sion on Locust Street in Kansas City. Emily resumed playing basketball as a guard for Sion for the 1928–1929 and 1929–1930 seasons, was captain of the junior and senior basketball teams, was secretary and treasurer of the junior class (Susie Schmid was president), and was French editor of the school newsletter *Echos Sioniens*. She boarded at Notre Dame de Sion during her senior year, the only time in twelve years that she decided to do this.

A big change in the way in which she played basketball occurred during Emily's senior year (1929–1930), as explained in *Echos Sioniens* (Volume VII, Number 1, fall 1929:

> The old three-court basketball is being replaced by a new and speedier type, namely the two-court game. Three-court and two-court basketball resemble each other much in that the players of yesterday greatly resemble the players of today. Yesterday, girls wore long skirts which restricted their movements; gradually the more modern and intelligent girl realized how much more practical shorter skirts would be. The skirts have become shorter and shorter by degrees, until the basketball costume has finally reached the present state of middies and bloomers (and, in some places, shorts).
>
> In the three-court game, there are three groups of players, each group restricted to its own limited space; whereas, in the new type, the middle court is entirely done away with. This affords more room, better team work, faster playing, and a better, more interesting game. It is prophesied that the new game will eventually give way to a single court form, however, this remains to be seen; in the mean time, let's put all we have into our new type of basketball.

Wohelo director Halsey Gulick visited the campers and their families in their homes during the winter of 1928–1929. He wrote in *The Wohelo Bird 1928* in anticipation of these trips, as follows:

> During the winter I hope to see most of you in your homes. I'll have the motion pictures that were taken during the summer and I hope you will want your friends to see them. Wohelo has always depended upon old campers in filling the vacancies. It is very unusual for a girl to come to camp who is not a personal friend of some one who is here or has been here. I hope it will always be this way. We want your friends.

Halsey visited the Sophians at Georgian Court, as evidenced by an undated note Estelle wrote to Emily while Emily was on a retreat with the Sion sisters:

> Tuesday
> Dearest Em:
>   Halsey came in town to-day and is coming for dinner this evening. If the retreat is over by this evening I know you will want to come home to see him. Let me know when to send the car for you.
>   Hope you have enjoyed your experience and are feeling well.
>   Heaps of love,
>   Mother.

Emily returned to Wohelo for the 1929 summer term, although no letters and few camp materials survive from that time.

In 1930 Emily graduated cum laude from Notre Dame de Sion and received the Gold Medal for "Sportsmanship." This award was something new. A short article in *Echos Sioniens* (Volume VII, Number 1, fall 1929) described the new award:

> The Senior class is offering, at the end of the year, a small gold basketball to the best all around "Sport." This does not necessarily mean the best player in the various sports; but the one who does not give way to feeling, "who can meet with triumph and disaster and treat them just the same," who thinks of her fellow classmates, and who at all times, both in and out of class, gives examples of Sionian spirit. Are you competing?

Emily matriculated at Smith College in the autumn of 1930 and was a member of the forty-six person contingent of Smith students who traveled to France for their junior year abroad in 1932–1933. She left Smith College in 1933 to attend the University of Missouri at Columbia where she studied writing and journalism. She joined the staff of the *Kansas City Star* in 1934 where she met her future husband Theodore Morgan O'Leary. Their marriage lasted fifty-eight years and yielded two sons, one of whom co-authored this book.

Entrance to brand-new campus of Notre Dame de Sion, Locust Street, Kansas City, Missouri, 1928. Emily Sophian began her junior year of high school here in September 1928. Image credit: Notre Dame de Sion Archives, Kansas City, Missouri.

Basketball team, Notre Dame de Sion School, Kansas City, Missouri, 1928. Emily Sophian is second from the left. Image credit: Notre Dame de Sion Archives, Kansas City, Missouri.

Footnotes

Chapter One:

1. William Harvey King: *History of Homeopathy and its Institutions in America*, Volume IV. New York City, New York: Lewis Publishing Company, 1905, p. 181.

2. Mark Wischnitzer: *To Dwell in Safety: The Story of Jewish Migration Since 1800*. Philadelphia, Pennsylvania: The Jewish Publication Society of America, 1949.

3. John D. Klier and Shlomo Lambroza: *Pogroms: Anti-Jewish Violence in Modern Russian History*. Cambridge, England: Cambridge University Press, 1992.

4. Morris Bishop: *A History of Cornell*. Ithaca, New York: Cornell University Press, 1962.

5. Medical Center Archives: "Establishment of New York Hospital-Cornell Medical Center," 2007 (five pages). Available at http://www.med.cornell.edu/archives/75years/site/pdf/historical_timeline.pdf; accessed April 1, 2011.

6. Arthur H. Aufses, Jr. and Barbara Hiss: *This House of Noble Deeds: The Mount Sinai Hospital, 1852–2002*. New York City, New York: New York University Press, 2002.

7. Wade W. Oliver: *The Man Who Lived for Tomorrow: A Biography of William Hallock Park, MD*. New York City, New York: E.P. Dutton & Company, 1941.

8. "Texas Gifts to Dr. Sophian: Grateful to Rockefeller Institute Specialist for Fighting Meningitis." Special to *New York Times*, Feb. 4, 1912, p. 14.

9. "Back from Winning War on Meningitis: Dr. Sophian Reports Epidemic in Dallas and Other Texas Cities Practically Stamped Out." *The New York Times*, February 15, 1912.

10. "Dr. Abraham Sophian, retired Kansas City physician dies at 71, since October the authority on infectious diseases had lived in Miami." *Kansas City Times*, Friday, September 20, 1957.

11. "Harry S. Sophian: Brother of Dr. A. Sophian had been ill ten months." *Kansas City Times*, September 22, 1945.

12. Harry J. Sophian built the Georgian Court Apartments at 400 E. Armour Boulevard in the Hyde Park neighborhood of Kansas City, Missouri at a cost of $300,000 around 1917-1918. By the early 1970s the Georgian Court Apartments had become unfashionable and were designated Section 8 low-income housing. In June 2006, the Maine-based firm Eagle Point Enterprises LLC announced plans to renovate and upgrade the Georgian Court. The project consisted of complete interior demolition and historic restoration of some interior and exterior features. The architect for the historic renovation was Rosemann & Associates and the contractor was Straub Construction Company. The building reopened in 2007. Source: Beth Paulsen: "Georgian Court Apartments grand opening." *Kansas City Star*. September 12, 2007. Available at http://pressreleases.kcstar.com/?q=node/3368; accessed April 1, 2011.

13. Harry Sophian also built Sophian Plaza (Kansas City) and Sophian Plaza (Tulsa, Oklahoma). See US Department of the Interior, National Park Service, National Register of Historic Places Inventory: Historic Sophian Plaza, 4618 Warwick Blvd, Kansas City." Available at http://dnr.mo.gov/shpo/nps-nr/83001019.pdf; accessed April 1, 2011; "New million dollar apartment building to be an imposing structure of Italian architecture." *Kansas City Star*, April 9, 1922, p. 2B; Nodia Case: "The Sophian Plaza: Enduring elegance in apartment living." *Historic Kansas City News* (Magazine), August 1978, Volume 3, Issue 1. See http://www.kchistory.org/cdm4/item_viewer. php?CISOROOT=/Local&CISOPTR=11304&CISOBOX=1 &REC=13; accessed March 14, 2010; and Diagram of Sophian Plaza, designed by Shepard and Wiser architects, is available at http://www.kcmo.org/idc/groups/cityplanningplanningdiv/ documents/cityplanninganddevelopment/017987.pdf; accessed April 1, 2011.

14. Robert E. Adams: "Research Hospital and how it grew." *Jackson County Medical Society Commemorative Section, Weekly Bulletin Golden Anniversary*, June 30, 1957.

15. Robert A. Long was a millionaire lumbar baron and Kansas City father who was a driving force behind creation of Kansas City's Liberty Memorial, a World War I museum and monument, and founder of Longview, a planned community in Washington state

dedicated in 1923. See Lenore K. Bradley: *Robert Alexander Long: A Lumber Baron of the Gilded Age.* Durham, North Carolina: Forest History Society, 1989; and "Robert Alexander Long" in William E. Connelley: *A Standard History of Kansas and Kansans.* Chicago, Illinois: Lewis Publishing Company, 1918. Available at http://skyways.lib.ks.us/genweb/archives/1918ks/biol/longra. html; accessed March 24, 2010.

16. Thomas Pendergast was a Kansas City and Jackson County (Missouri) Democratic political boss who eventually served time for income tax evasion at the U.S. Penitentiary in Leavenworth, Kansas. Many books have been written about him, including 1) Lawrence H. Larsen: *Pendergast!* Columbia, Missouri: University of Missouri Press, 1997; 2) William M. Reddig: *Toms' Town: Kansas City and the Pendergast Legend.* Raleigh, North Carolina: C and M Online, 1986; 3) Frank R. Hayde: *The Mafia and the Machine: The Story of the Kansas City Mob.* Fort Lee, New Jersey: Barricade Books, 2008; 4) Rudolph H. Hartmann and Robert H. Ferrell: *The Kansas City Investigation: Pendergast's Downfall, 1938-1939.* Columbia, Missouri: University of Missouri Press, 1999; and 5) Robert H. Ferrell: *Truman and Pendergast.* Columbia, Missouri: University of Missouri Press, 1999.

17. "The Great Pandemic. The United States in 1918–1919." United States Department of Public Health. Available at http://1918. pandemicflu.gov/your_state/missouri.htm; accessed April 1, 2011.

18. Alfred W. Crosby: *America's Forgotten Pandemic: The Influenza of 1918.* Cambridge, England: Cambridge University Press, 2003, p. 19.

19. Susan Debra Sykes Berry: "Politics and Pandemic in 1918 Kansas City." Kansas City, Missouri, 2010. Available at https:// mospace.umsystem.edu/xmlui/bitstream/handle/10355/7521/ SykesBerryThesisPolPan.pdf?sequence=1; accessed April 1, 2011.

20. *A Nineteenth Century Miracle: the Brothers Ratisbonne and the Congregation of Notre Dame de Sion.* Translated from the French by L. M. Leggatt. London, England: Burns Oates & Washbourne, 1922.

21. *Origins of Sion: Théodore Ratisbonne: Memoirs.* Translated by Sister Marian Dolan from the French edition of 1966 containing a long introduction of Mother Marie Alice and the

text of Father Théodore's Memoirs. Available at http://www. salvationisfromthejews.com/TRM.pdf; accessed April 1, 2011.

22. Sister Marie Ida de Sion: *Sion! Long May Her Banner Wave! Memories of Notre Dame de Sion in Kansas City 1912–1965 and the Fifty Golden Years of Sister Marie Ida de Sion 1915–1965.* Kansas City, Missouri: April 22, 1965. (Book is not paginated).

23. Frank J. Adler: *Roots in a Moving Stream: The Centennial History of Congregation B'nai Jehudah of Kansas City 1870-1970.* Kansas City, Missouri: The Temple, Congregation B'nai Jehudah, 1972. See also Samuel S. Mayerberg: *Chronicle of an American Crusader.* Mayerberg Press, 2007.

24. Nathan Glazer: *American Judaism: An Historical Survey of the Jewish Religion in America.* Chicago, Illinois: University of Chicago Press Press, 1957, pp. 46-48, pp. 60-61. See also David Philipson: *The Reform movement in Judaism* first published in 1903 and revised by Philipson in 1931 (New York: MacMillan). It covers the Reform movement from its beginnings up until 1930. See also Michael A. Meyer: *Response to Modernity: A History of the Reform Movement in Judaism.* Detroit, Michigan: Wayne State University Press, 1988. It covers the Reform movement from 1931 to the 1970s.

25. The Ruth Fielding series of thirty books was written by "Alice B. Emerson," a pseudonym for W. Bert Foster (volumes 1–19), Elizabeth M. Duffield Ward (volumes 20–22), and Mildred A. Wirt Benson (volumes 23–30). The series was published by Cupples and Leon from 1913 through 1934. Ruth Fielding was a strong-willed young woman and was also a career woman. For more information on the Ruth Fielding series, see http://www. series-books.com/ruthfielding/ruthfielding.html; accessed April 1, 2011.

26. The Bobbsey Twins series of seventy-two books was written by "Laura Lee Hope," a pseudonym for many writers. The series was published by Stratemeyer Syndicate owned by Edward Stratemeyer 1904 through 1979. For more information on the Bobbsey Twins series, see James D. Keeline: "The Writers of the Bobbsey Series," August 25, 1999, available at http://pwl. netcom.com/~drmike99/Keeline.html; accessed April 1, 2011; and James D. Keeline: "Bobbsey Twins Formats"; accessed April 1, 2011.

Chapter Two:

1. Wohelo and Timanous camps continue to operate today. Descendants of Luther and Charlotte Gulick operate Wohelo. For more information, see http://www.wohelo.com/ and http://www.camptimanous.com/ accessed March 22, 2011.

2. Herbert G. Jones: *Sebago Lake Land*. Freeport, Maine: Cumberland Press, 1949, pp. 10–11, 16.

3. "Why is Sebago so deep?" Maine Geological Survey, State of Maine, Department of Conservation. Available at http://www.maine.gov/doc/nrimc/mgs/explore/lakes/sites/feb99.htm; accessed March 24, 2011.

4. Colin G. Calloway: *The Western Abenakis of Vermont, 1600-1800: War, Migration, and the Survival of an Indian People*. Norman, Oklahoma: University of Oklahoma Press, 1994. See also Colin G. Calloway: *The American Revolution in Indian Country: Crisis and Diversity in Native American Communities*. Cambridge, England: Cambridge University Press, 1995.

5. Benjamin Woodbridge Dwight: *The History of the Descendants of Elder John Strong, of Northampton, Massachusetts*. Albany, New York: Joel Munsell, 1871, Volume II, p. 1142.

6. Albert Dexter Rust: *Record of the Rust Family*: Waco, Texas: Published by the Author, 1891, p. 315.

7. Robert Samuel Fletcher: *History of Oberlin College: From its Foundation through the Civil War*. Two volumes. Oberlin, Ohio: Oberlin College Press, 1943.

8. Geoffrey Blodgett: *Oberlin History: Essays and Impressions*. Kent, Ohio: Kent State University Press, 2006.

9. "Oberlin College Graduate School of Theology (1833–1966)." In Oberlin College Archives. Available at http://www.oberlin.edu/archive/holdings/finding/RG11/adminhist.html; accessed March 22, 2011.

10. Roland M. Baumann: *Constructing Black Education at Oberlin College*. Athens, Ohio: Ohio University Press, 2010.

11. "5th Regiment Cavalry United States Colored Troops." Available at http://home.comcast.net/~5thuscc/; accessed March 22, 2011.

12. "The American Home Missionary Society Papers, 1816–1894." Available at http://www.gale.cengage.com/servlet/ItemDetailSe rvlet?region=9&imprint=000&cf=n&titleCode=SR755&type= 4&id=D3621; accessed March 22, 2011. See also "Archives: The American Home Missionary Society," Billy Graham Center,

Wheaton College, Wheaton, Illinois. Available at http://www. wheaton.edu/bgc/archives/GUIDES/142.htm; accessed March 22, 2011.

13. *The Home Missionary for the Year Ending April 1863.* Volume XXXV, New York City, New York: American Home Missionary Society, 1863, pp. 98, 273.

14. *The Home Missionary for the Year Ending April, 1886.* Volume LVIII. New York City, New York: American Home Missionary Society, 1886, p. 197.

15. See "Miller County Museum & Historical Society: Churches of Miller County; The Congregational Church." Available at http://www.millercountymuseum.org/congregational.html; accessed March 22, 2011.

16. The history that Luther and Charlotte met at a Drury College river party is from Charlotte Gulick Hewson: *Wohelo 1907–1930.* South Casco, Maine: Wohelo Press, 2000, p. 21. The history that they met while camping is from Ethel Josephine Dorgan: *Luther Halsey Gulick, 1865–1918.* New York City, New York: Bureau of Publications, Teachers College, Columbia University, 1934, pp. 8–9. For additional well-written biographical information on Luther Halsey Gulick, Jr., see "Luther Halsey Gulick Papers, 1853–1992" at Springfield College Archives and Special Collections, Springfield, Massachusetts, Manuscript Number MS 503. Available at http://www.spfldcol.edu/homepage/library.nsf/5331A8EF3D10C0A9852576550051B0B1/$File/MS%20503%20Luther%20Halsey%20Gulick%20Papers%20-%20Finding%20Aid.pdf; accessed March 23, 2011.

17. The term *Micronesia* was first proposed in 1831 by French explorer Jules Dumont d'Urville (1790–1842) to describe the thousands of small islands west of the Hawaiian Islands, in the western Pacific Ocean.

18. Sidney Ahlstrom: *A Religious History of the American People.* New Haven, Connecticut: Yale University Press, 1972.

19. Amanda Porterfield: *American Religious History.* Oxford, England: Blackwell Publishers, 2002.

20. Edwin Guastad and Leigh Schmidt: *The Religious History of America.* New York City, New York: HarperOne, 2004.

21. Ethel Josephine Dorgan: *Luther Halsey Gulick, 1865–1918.* New York City, New York: Bureau of Publications, Teachers College, Columbia University, 1934, pp. 3–7.

22. "Frank Fanning Jewett." In *General Catalogue of Oberlin College, 1833–1908*. Oberlin, Ohio: Oberlin College Press, 1909, p. 155. See also American Chemical Society: National Historic Chemical Landmarks: "Production of aluminum metal by electrochemistry." Available at http://acswebcontent.acs.org/landmarks/landmarks/cmh/index.html; accessed March 22, 2011.

23. Geoffrey Blodgett: *Oberlin Architecture, College and Town*. Kent, Ohio: Kent State University Press, 1985.

24. Ethel Josephine Dorgan: *Luther Halsey Gulick, 1865–1918*. New York City, New York: Bureau of Publications, Teachers College, Columbia University, 1934, p. 1.

25. For more information on Dr. Dudley Sargent, see "Dr. Thomas chats with Dr. Dudley Sargent." Available at http://www.ihpra.org/sargent_chat.htm; accessed March 22, 2011. Dr. Sargent wrote many books, including *Physical Education* (Boston, Massachusetts: Ginn & Company, 1906) and *Dudley Allen Sargent: An Autobiography* (Philadelphia, Pennsylvania: Lea and Febiger, 1927).

26. Elmer L. Johnson: *The History of YMCA Physical Education*. Chicago, Illinois: Association Press, 1979, p. 56.

27. J. E. Hodder-Williams: *The Father of the Red Triangle: The Life of Sir George Williams, Founder of the Y. M. C. A.* London, England: Hodder and Stoughton, 1918. See also Elmer L. Johnson: *The History of YMCA Physical Education*. Chicago, Illinois: Association Press, 1979; and "Young Men's Christian Association of Greater Boston records," Archives and Special Collections of Northeastern University, available at http://www.lib.neu.edu/archives/collect/findaids/m13find.htm; accessed March 27, 2011.

28. Claude Edwin Heaton: *A Historical Sketch: New York University College of Medicine, 1841–1941*. New York City, New York: New York University Press, 1941, p. 21.

29. "School for Christian Workers. *New York Times*, November 27, 1884. See also Ethel Josephine Dorgan: *Luther Halsey Gulick, 1865–1918*. New York City, New York: Bureau of Publications, Teachers College, Columbia University, 1934, pp. 5–7.

30. Elmer L. Johnson: *The History of YMCA Physical Education*. Chicago, Illinois: Association Press, 1979, pp. 57–58.

31. Helen Buckler, Mary F. Fiedler, and Martha F. Allen: *Wo-He-Lo: The Story of Camp Fire Girls 1910–1960.* New York City, New York: Holt, Rinehart and Winston, 1961, p. 12.

32. Charlotte Gulick Hewson: *Wohelo 1907–1930.* South Casco, Maine: Wohelo Press, 2000, pp. 22,29.

33. John Donald Gustav-Wrathall: *Take the Young Stranger by the Hand: Same-Sex Relations and the YMCA.* Chicago, Illinois: University of Chicago Press, 1998, p. 24.

34. "Trains Young Christians; An Institution in Springfield Which is Doing a Great Work; Well Equipped for its Purpose; 'Tis a Normal College to Prepare Competent Officers for Young Men's Christian Associations – The Gymnasium." *New York Times,* December 29, 1895.

35. *Basketball Was Born Here.* Springfield College online book (17 pages). Available at http://content.yudu.com/Library/A1rdir/ BasketballWasBornHer/resources/index.htm?referrerUrl=h ttp%3A%2F%2Fwww.spfldcol.edu%2Fhome.nsf%2FThe-Birthplace-of-Basketball-test; accessed March 22, 2011. See also "Springfield College: The Birthplace of Basketball." Available at http://www.spfldcol.edu/home.nsf/The-Birthplace-of-Basketball; accessed March 22, 2011.

36. "Basket Ball Popular; Progress of the Game Started Eleven Years Ago. It Was First a Y. M. C. A. Sport, and Is Now Played by All Classes of Athletes." *New York Times,* December 23, 1902. See also "Basketball's Inventor; Reader Says Dr. Gulick Rates Credit, Not Dr. Naismith." In Letters to the Sports Editor. *New York Times,* June 13, 1942.

37. Elmer L. Johnson: *The History of YMCA Physical Education.* Chicago, Illinois: Association Press, 1979, p. 90.

38. Ralph Melnick: *Senda Berenson: The Unlikely Founder of Women's Basketball.* Amherst, Massachusetts: University of Massachusetts Press, 2007, pp. 2–3. See also "Senda Berenson Papers, 1875 – 1996 (bulk 1890–1952). Five College (Massachusetts) Archives Digital Access Project. Available at http://clio.fivecolleges.edu/ smith/berenson/; accessed April 2, 2011. See also Sally Jenkins: "History of Women's Basketball: From Berenson to Bolton, Women's Hoops Has Been Rising for 100 Years." Available at http://www.wnba.com/about_us/jenkins_feature.html; April 5, 2011.

39. Edward Marshall: "To Help the Tragic Army of Failures in Schools; There are 250,000 of Them and Dr. Luther H. Gulick

of the Russell Sage Foundation Tells What Is Being Done to Remedy Conditions." *New York Times*, April 2, 1911.

40. David C. Scott and Brendan Murphy: *The Scouting Party: Pioneering and Preservation, Progressivism and Preparedness in the Boy Scouts of America*. Irving, Texas: Red Honor Press, 2010.

41. Edward Marshall: "Girls Take Up the Boy Scout Idea and Band Together: Campfire Girls of America Is the Name of a New Organization Begun by Mrs. Luther Gulick and Backed by Many influential Social Workers to Make Better Women in the Future." *New York Times*, March 17, 1912.

42. Ethel Josephine Dorgan: *Luther Halsey Gulick, 1865–1918*. New York City, New York: Bureau of Publications, Teachers College, Columbia University, 1934, pages 155–171.

43. Ibid, p. 23. Louise Gulick married Horace Eddy Robinson in 1912. Katharine married Arthur Edward Hamilton in 1916. They divorced and she married Allen Blair Curtis. Halsey married Gretchen Messer in 1924. They divorced and he married Dorothy Merrill, a former camper and counselor, in 1931. For more information on Louise, see her obituary titled, "Mrs. Horace E. Robinson" in the *New York Times* on June 28, 1941. For more information on Frances, see her obituary titled "Miss Frances J. Gulick; Won Citation in World War—Parents Founded Camp Fire Girls" in the *New York Times on* November 26, 1936.

44. Scholars have begun to analyze the history of the American camping movement. Examples are: Paula Fass and Marta Gutman: *Designing Modern Childhoods: History, Space, and the Material Culture of Children.* (New Brunswick, New Jersey: Rutgers University Press, 2008); Laurie Susan Kahn: *Sleepaway: The Girls of Summer and the Camps They Love.* (New York City, New York: Workman Publishing Company, 2003); Susan A. Miller: *Growing Girls: The Natural Origins of Girls' Organizations in America.* (New Brunswick, New Jersey: Rutgers University Press, 2007); and Leslie Paris: *Children's Nature: The Rise of the American Summer Camp.* New York City, New York: New York University Press, 2010.

45. Ethel Josephine Dorgan: *Luther Halsey Gulick, 1865–1918*. New York City, New York: Bureau of Publications, Teachers College, Columbia University, 1934, pp. 15–17.

46. Ethel Rogers: *Sebago-Wohelo Camp Fire Girls*. Battle Creek, Michigan: Good Health Publishing Company, 1915, p. 13. See also Helen Buckler, Mary F. Fiedler, and Martha F. Allen: *Wo-*

He-Lo: The Story of Camp Fire Girls 1910–1960. New York City, New York: Holt, Rinehart and Winston, 1961, p. 10.

47. Charlotte Vetter Gulick: *Emergencies.* Boston, Massachusetts: Ginn and Company, 1909, pp. 121–122.

48. Helen Buckler, Mary F. Fiedler, and Martha F. Allen: *Wo-He-Lo: The Story of Camp Fire Girls 1910–1960.* New York City, New York: Holt, Rinehart and Winston, 1961, pp. 11–13.

49. Ethel Josephine Dorgan: *Luther Halsey Gulick, 1865–1918.* New York City, New York: Bureau of Publications, Teachers College, Columbia University, 1934, p. 24.

50. Charlotte Gulick Hewson: *Wohelo 1907–1930.* South Casco, Maine: Wohelo Press, 2000, pp. 24–25.

51. Peter C. English: *Rheumatic Fever in America and Britain: A Biological, Epidemiological, and Medical History.* New Brunswick, New Jersey: Rutgers University Press, 1999. See also Benedict F. Massell: *Rheumatic Fever and Streptococcal Infection.* Boston, Massachusetts: Boston Medical Library Press (Countway Library of Medicine), 1997.

52. Brian Morris: *Ernest Thompson Seton: Founder of the Woodcraft Indian Movement 1860–1946; Apostle of Indian Wisdom and Pioneer Ecologist.* Lewiston, New York: Edwin Mellen Press, 2007. See also Ernest Thompson Seton: *Woodcraft and Indian Lore.* New York City, New York: Skyhorse Publishing, 2007.

53. Helen Buckler, Mary F. Fiedler, and Martha F. Allen: *Wo-He-Lo: The Story of Camp Fire Girls 1910–1960.* New York City, New York: Holt, Rinehart and Winston, 1961, p. 15.

54. Ethel Josephine Dorgan: *Luther Halsey Gulick, 1865–1918.* New York City, New York: Bureau of Publications, Teachers College, Columbia University, 1934, pp. 26–27.

55. Helen Buckler, Mary F. Fiedler, and Martha F. Allen: *Wo-He-Lo: The Story of Camp Fire Girls 1910–1960.* New York City, New York: Holt, Rinehart and Winston, 1961, pp. pp. 195–203.

56. Ethel Josephine Dorgan: *Luther Halsey Gulick, 1865–1918.* New York City, New York: Bureau of Publications, Teachers College, Columbia University, 1934, pp. 147–148. See also Gulick's obituary titled, "Dr. Luther H. Gulick, Educator, Is Dead; Director of Physical Education in New York Schools, Expires in Maine Camp." *New York Times,* August 14, 1918.

57. Helen Buckler, Mary F. Fiedler, and Martha F. Allen: *Wo-He-Lo: The Story of Camp Fire Girls 1910–1960.* New York City, New York: Holt, Rinehart and Winston, 1961, pp. 159, 160–162.

58. Charlotte Gulick Hewson: *Wohelo 1907–1930*. South Casco, Maine: Wohelo Press, 2000, p. 124

59. Ibid, p. 62.

60. Lehigh Coaches Awaited; Three Places Still Open on Staff as Others Are Reappointed." *New York Times*, September 26, 1926.

61. "Gulick Resigns at Lehigh." *New York Times*, January, 1927.

62. "Joseph E. Raycroft Papers, 1888–1953." Princeton University Library Mudd Manuscript Library. Available at http://diglib. princeton.edu/ead/getEad?eadid=AC146&kw=; accessed March 24, 2011.

63. "J. Halsey Gulick 1899–1980." Available at http://mainecamps. org/wp-content/blogs.dir/3/files/file/2010GulickAwardBooklet. pdf; accessed March 24, 2011. The short biography at this website reads:

J. Halsey Gulick, educator, public servant, and outdoorsman, was devoted to organized youth camping and particularly to camps in Maine. He was one of the first camping leaders to call attention to the value of youth camps to the economy of the states.

In the fall of 1934 Gulick was elected President of the New England Camping Association which was the start of many years of volunteer leadership in camping's professional organizations including the Maine Camp Directors Association. In 1982, the Maine Camp Directors Association created the Halsey Gulick Award to recognize other leaders who have given distinguished service to the camping movement in Maine.

Mr. Gulick was one of very few independent camp directors of his day to reside in the state of Maine. As the son of Dr. Luther Gulick, founder of the Luther Gulick Camps, he was part of a very small group to be educated with the idea that conducting recreational summer camps for children was a bona fide role for a professional educator.

Halsey's parents, Dr. and Mrs. Luther Gulick, were pioneers of the camping movement. They began the first camp at Gale's Ferry, CT., in 1888. That camp was [dis]continued in 1906 when they began the Luther Gulick Camps in South Casco, Maine on Sebago Lake. Luther Gulick died during the summer of 1918 due to a strenuous winter of investigating overseas work of the Y. M. C. A. Mrs. Gulick carried on the camps until her death in 1928 at which time Halsey became director.

Halsey was educated at the Ethical Culture School in New York, Phillips Exeter Academy, and Princeton University, graduating in 1923. He taught physical education at Lehigh University from 1923–1927 and at Princeton from 1928–1929. Mr. Gulick headed the physical education department at the Fessenden School for Boys in Massachusetts from 1931–33. In 1933 he became the director of the junior division of the Mary C. Wheeler School in Providence.

In 1935, Gulick was appointed Headmaster at Proctor Academy in New Hampshire where he served with distinction for 17 years. In 1953, he left the independent school to devote his full time to the Luther Gulick Camps.

Mr. Gulick had many interests including all forms of outdoor sports like swimming, fishing, motorboat racing [see one of Emily's letters], and skiing. In 1931 he was married to Dorothy Merrill, from Washington, DC. Together, they directed the camps until the late 1960s, when they turned the day-to-day operations over to their three daughters.

Halsey's daughter Louise Van Winkle and her husband, Davis Van Winkle, directed Camp Wohelo, the Luther Gulick Camps for over 34 years. They now serve as Directors Emeriti.

Their children Heidi and Mark, and Mark's wife Quincy, are now the Directors of Wohelo. There are over 5000 alumni of the camps. Many of the older generation of campers and parents have known all members of the Gulick family.

Chapter Three:
1. Charlotte Gulick Hewson: *Wohelo 1907–1930*. South Casco, Maine: Wohelo Press, 2000, p. 107.
2. Ibid, p. 29.

Chapter Four:
1. The Morrison Hotel was considered one of Chicago's finest hotels during the twentieth century until it was razed in 1965. It boasted two restaurants—the Boston Oyster House and the Terrace Garden dinner theater where Emily ate the night she arrived in Chicago. For more information on Morrison Hotel, see http://chicago.urban-history.org/sites/hotels/morrison.htm; accessed April 1, 2011.
2. Charlotte Gulick Hewson: *Wohelo 1907–1930*. South Casco, Maine: Wohelo Press, 2000, p. 69.

3. Herbert G. Jones: *Sebago Lake Land*. Freeport, Maine: Cumberland Press, 1949, pp. 46, 53.
4. Ibid, pp. 10, 103–104. See also Diane Barnes and Jack Barnes: *Sebago Lake Area: Windham, Standish, Raymond, Casco, Sebago, and Naples*. Charleston, South Carolina: Arcadia Publishing, 1996, p. 66. See also Brenda Wineapple: *Hawthorne: A Life*. New York City, New York: Random House, 2003, pp. 32–36.
5. Moses Foster Sweetser: *The White Mountains: A Handbook for Travellers* [*sic*]. Boston, Massachusetts: James R. Osgood and Company, 1881, pp. 402–403.
6. Luther H. Gulick: *Exercise and Rest*. New York City, New York: Reprinted from The North American Review, October, 1910 by the Department of Child Hygiene of the Russell Sage Foundation, 1910, p. 5.
7. Luther H. Gulick: "The social function of play." In *Journal of Education*, Volume 81, June 3, 1915, p. 598. "The Art of Dancing; Dr. Luther H. Gulick Advocates Folk-Dances as Conducive to Physical and Moral Health." *New York Times*, November 12, 1910.
8. Charlotte Gulick Hewson: *Wohelo 1907–1930*. South Casco, Maine: Wohelo Press, 2000, p. 78.
9. The long history of Oakwood Country Club is available at http://www.oakwoodcountryclub.org/history_beg.html; accessed April 1, 2011.
10. "Physician takes airplane to reach sick boy." *Galveston Daily News*, April 22, 1928, p. 15.
11. Rod Simpson: *Airlife's World Aircraft*. Shrewsbury, England: Airlife Publishing, 2001, p. 518.
12. Ibid, p. 517.
13. "3 Pilots and 3 Passengers Dead in Air Accidents; Army Man Killed in Old Plane; Two Other planes of Same Make Take Fire." *Waterloo Evening Courier*, August 1, 1927, p. 2.
14. The description of the purchased land is a document received on January 21, 1930 by the International Joint Commission, United States and Canada, and is available at http://www.ijc.org/php/publications/pdf/ID187.pdf; accessed March 24, 2011.
15. The full text of the Reclamation Act/Newlands Act of 1902 is available at http://www.ccrh.org/comm/umatilla/primary/newlands.htm; accessed March 25, 2011.
16. "The Beginnings of Agriculture in Washington State." Washington State Agricultural Bibliography, University of

Washington University Libraries. Available at http://www.lib. washington.edu/preservation/projects/washag/ag.html; accessed March 24, 2011.

17. *Irrigated Lands of the State of Washington*. Washington (State) Bureau of Statistics and Immigration. Ann Arbor, Michigan: University of Michigan Press, 1910, p. 39.

18. The text of the "1937 Trail Smelter Case (TRAIL)" is available at http://www1.american.edu/ted/TRAIL.HTM; accessed March 25, 2011. For the history of the Trail smelter before it was purchased by Consolidated Mining & Smelting Company of Canada, Ltd. in 1906, see Elsie Turnbull: *Trail: A Smelter City*. Langley, British Columbia: Sunfire Publications, 1985.

19. Arne Kaijser: "The Trail from Trail: New challenges for historians of technology." *E-Technology and Culture*, 2011. Available at http://etc.technologyandculture.net/2011/02/the-trail-from-trail/; accessed March 25, 2011.

20. James R. Allum: "'An Outcrop of Hell: History, Environment, and the Politics of the Trail Smelter Dispute." In *Transboundary Harm in International Law: Lessons from the Trail Smelter Arbitration*. Rebecca Bratspies and Russell Miller (eds.). Cambridge, England, 2006, pp. 13–26.

21. Keith A. Murray: "The Trail Smelter Case: International Air Pollution in the Columbia Valley." *British Columbia Studies*. Volume 15, 1972, pp. 68–85. Available at ojs.library.ubc.ca/index.php/bcstudies/article/download/757/799; accessed March 25, 2011. Murray's worthwhile article charts the economic history of the Upper Columbia River region.

22. Alan Williams: *Republic of Images: A History of French Filmmaking*. Cambridge, Massachusetts: Harvard University Press, 1992.

23. Raymond Fielding: *The American Newsreel 1911–1967*. Second edition. Jefferson, North Carolina: McFarland & Company, 2006.

24. The silent Wohelo film is available at http://www.filmpreservation.org/preserved-films/screening-room/wohelo-camp-ca-1919; accessed March 25, 2011.

25. Herbert G. Jones: *Sebago Lake Land*. Freeport, Maine: Cumberland Press, 1949, p. 16.

26. "Up the Winding Songo River." *Chamber of Commerce Board of Trade Journal of Maine*, May 1909, Volume 22, Number 1, p. 67.

27. Henry Wadsworth Longfellow: "Songo River." *The Poetical Works of Henry Wadsworth Longfellow in Six Volumes.* Boston, Massachusetts: Houghton, Mifflin and Company, Volume III, p. 97.

28. Christoph Irmscher: *Public Poet, Private Man: Henry Wadsworth Longfellow at 200.* Amherst, Massachusetts: University of Massachusetts, 2009.

29. Source: *Wohelo Songbook.* Available at http://www.wohelo.com/wp-content/uploads/2010/02/TG-songbook-05_Finished.pdf; accessed March 6, 2011.

30. Old Chief Timanous lyrics are available at *Wohelo Songbook* at http://www.wohelo.com/wp-content/uploads/2010/02/TG-songbook-05_Finished.pdf; accessed March 6, 2011.

31. Herbert G. Jones: *Sebago Lake Land.* Freeport, Maine: Cumberland Press, 1949, p. 12.

32. The Medici Fountain in the Luxembourg Garden is located in the 6th arrondissement in Paris. It was built about 1630 by Marie de Medici, widow of the French king, Henry IV, who was born a Huguenot (French Protestant Calvinist) and converted to Catholicism to gain the crown. He stopped the Wars of Religion between the French Catholics and French Protestants. For all his trouble, this remarkable king was assassinated by a French Catholic fanatic in 1610. Henry IV was the first of the Bourbon kings. Marie de Medici was regent for their then nine-year-old son, King Louis XIII of France, until 1617. The Medici Fountain was moved to its present location and extensively rebuilt from 1864 to 1866.

References

Robert E. Adams: "Research Hospital and how it grew." *Jackson County Medical Society Commemorative Section, Weekly Bulletin Golden Anniversary,* June 30, 1957.

Frank J. Adler: *Roots in a Moving Stream: The Centennial History of Congregation B'nai Jehudah of Kansas City 1870-1970.* Kansas City, Missouri: The Temple, Congregation B'nai Jehudah, 1972.

Sidney Ahlstrom: *A Religious History of the American People.* New Haven, Connecticut: Yale University Press, 1972.

James R. Allum: "'An Outcrop of Hell: History, Environment, and the Politics of the Trail Smelter Dispute." In *Transboundary Harm in International Law: Lessons from the Trail Smelter Arbitration.* Rebecca Bratspies and Russell Miller (eds.). Cambridge, England, 2006, pp. 13–26.

Arthur H. Aufses, Jr. and Barbara Hiss: *This House of Noble Deeds: The Mount Sinai Hospital, 1852–2002.* New York City, New York: New York University Press, 2002.

Diane Barnes and Jack Barnes: *Sebago Lake Area: Windham, Standish, Raymond, Casco, Sebago, and Naples.* Charleston, South Carolina: Arcadia Publishing, 1996.

Roland M. Baumann: *Constructing Black Education at Oberlin College.* Athens, Ohio: Ohio University Press, 2010.

Morris Bishop: *A History of Cornell.* Ithaca, New York: Cornell University Press, 1962.

Geoffrey Blodgett: *Oberlin Architecture, College and Town.* Kent, Ohio: Kent State University Press, 1985.

Geoffrey Blodgett: *Oberlin History: Essays and Impressions.* Kent, Ohio: Kent State University Press, 2006.

Book of the Camp Fire Girls. New York City, New York: Camp Fire Girls, 1913.

Lenore K. Bradley: *Robert Alexander Long: A Lumber Baron of the Gilded Age.* Durham, North Carolina: Forest History Society, 1989.

Helen Buckler, Mary F. Fiedler, and Martha F. Allen: *Wo-He-Lo: The Story of Camp Fire Girls 1910–1960.* New York City, New York: Holt, Rinehart and Winston, 1961.

Colin G. Calloway: *The American Revolution in Indian Country: Crisis and Diversity in Native American Communities.* Cambridge, England: Cambridge University Press, 1995.

Colin G. Calloway: *The Western Abenakis of Vermont, 1600-1800: War, Migration, and the Survival of an Indian People.* Norman, Oklahoma: University of Oklahoma Press, 1994.

Alfred W. Crosby: *America's Forgotten Pandemic: The Influenza of 1918.* Cambridge, England: Cambridge University Press, 2003.

Ethel Josephine Dorgan: *Luther Halsey Gulick, 1865–1918.* New York City, New York: Bureau of Publications, Teachers College, Columbia University, 1934.

Benjamin Woodbridge Dwight: *The History of the Descendants of Elder John Strong of Northampton, Massachusetts.* Volume II. Albany, New York: Joel Munsell, 1871.

Peter C. English: *Rheumatic Fever in America and Britain: A Biological, Epidemiological, and Medical History.* New Brunswick, New Jersey: Rutgers University Press, 1999.

Paula Fass and Marta Gutman: *Designing Modern Childhoods: History, Space, and the Material Culture of Children.* New Brunswick, New Jersey: Rutgers University Press, 2008.

Raymond Fielding: *The American Newsreel 1911–1967.* Second edition. Jefferson, North Carolina: McFarland & Company, 2006.

Robert Samuel Fletcher: *History of Oberlin College: From its Foundation through the Civil War.* Two volumes. Oberlin, Ohio: Oberlin College Press, 1943.

Miriam Forman-Brunell: *Girlhood in America: An Encyclopedia*. Santa Barbara, California: ABC-CLIO, 2001.

Nathan Glazer: *American Judaism: An Historical Survey of the Jewish Religion in America*. Chicago: The University of Chicago Press, 1957.

Edwin Guastad and Leigh Schmidt: *The Religious History of America*. New York City, New York: HarperOne, 2004.

Charlotte Vetter Gulick: *Emergencies*. (Book Two of The Gulick Hygiene Series). Boston, Massachusetts: Ginn and Company, 1909.

Luther Halsey Gulick: *The Dynamic of Love*. New York City, New York: Association Press, 1917.

Luther Halsey Gulick: *The Dynamic of Manhood*: New York City, New York: Association Press, 1918.

Luther Halsey Gulick: *The Efficient Life*. Garden City, New York: Doubleday, Page & Company, 1907.

Luther Halsey Gulick: *The Gulick Hygiene Series*. (Editor). Boston, Massachusetts: Ginn and Company, 1906–1909. See also Frances Gulick Jewett and Charlotte Vetter Gulick entries.

Luther Halsey Gulick: *The Healthful Art of Dancing*. Garden City, New York: Doubleday, Page & Company, 1908.

Luther Halsey Gulick: *Manual of Physical Measurements in Connection with the Association Gymnasium Records*. New York City, New York: International Committee of the Y. M. C. A., 1892.

Luther Halsey Gulick: *Mind and Work*. Garden City, New York: Doubleday, Page & Company, 1908.

Luther Halsey Gulick: *Morals and Morale*. New York City, New York: Association Press, 1919. Published posthumously.

Luther Halsey Gulick: *A Philosophy of Play*. New York City, New York: Charles Scribner's Sons, 1920.

Luther Halsey Gulick: *Physical Education by Muscular Exercise*. Philadelphia, Pennsylvania: P. Blakiston's Son & Co., 1904.

Luther Halsey Gulick: *Ten Minutes' Exercise for Busy Men*. New York City, New York: Association Press, 1902.

Luther Halsey Gulick and James Naismith: *Basket Ball*. New York City, New York: American Sports Publishing Company, 1894.

Luther Halsey Gulick and Leonard P. Ayres: *Medical Inspection of Schools*. New York City, New York: Russell Sage Foundation, 1908.

Luther Halsey Gulick and Marion Florence Lansing: *Food and Life*. Boston, Massachusetts: Ginn and Company, 1920.

John Donald Gustav-Wrathall: *Take the Young Stranger by the Hand: Same-Sex Relations and the YMCA*. Chicago, Illinois: University of Chicago Press.

Claude Edwin Heaton: *A Historical Sketch: New York University College of Medicine, 1841–1941*. New York City, New York: New York University Press, 1941,

Charlotte Gulick Hewson: *Wohelo 1907–1930*. South Casco, Maine: Wohelo Press, 2000.

J. E. Hodder-Williams: *The Father of the Red Triangle: The Life of Sir George Williams, Founder of the Y. M. C. A.* London, England: Hodder and Stoughton, 1918.

The Home Missionary for the Year Ending April 1863. Volume XXXV, New York City, New York: American Home Missionary Society, 1863, pp. 98, 273.

The Home Missionary for the Year Ending April 1886. Volume LVIII. New York City, New York: American Home Missionary Society, 1886, p. 197.

Christoph Irmscher: *Public Poet, Private Man: Henry Wadsworth Longfellow at 200*. Amherst, Massachusetts: University of Massachusetts, 2009.

Irrigated Lands of the State of Washington. Washington (State) Bureau of Statistics and Immigration. Ann Arbor, Michigan: University of Michigan Press, 1910.

Frances Gulick Jewett: *The Body at Work*. (Book Four of The Gulick Hygiene Series). Boston, Massachusetts: Ginn and Company, 1909.

Frances Gulick Jewett: *Control of Body and Mind*. (Book Five of The Gulick Hygiene Series). Boston, Massachusetts: Ginn and Company, 1909.

Frances Gulick Jewett: *Good Health*. (Book One of The Gulick Hygiene Series). Boston, Massachusetts: Ginn and Company, 1906.

Frances Gulick Jewett: *Luther Halsey Gulick: Missionary in Hawaii, Micronesia, Japan, and China*. Boston, Massachusetts: The Pilgrim Press, 1895.

Frances Gulick Jewett: *Town and City*. (Book Three of The Gulick Hygiene Series.) Boston, Massachusetts: Ginn and Company, 1906.

Elmer L. Johnson: *The History of YMCA Physical Education*. Chicago, Illinois: Association Press, 1979.

Herbert G. Jones: *Sebago Lake Land*. Freeport, Maine: The Cumberland Press, 1949.

Laurie Susan Kahn: *Sleepaway: The Girls of Summer and the Camps They Love*. New York City, New York: Workman Publishing Company, 2003.

John D. Klier and Shlomo Lambroza: *Pogroms: Anti-Jewish Violence in Modern Russian History*. Cambridge, England: Cambridge University Press, 1992.

Lawrence H. Larsen: *Pendergast!* Columbia, Missouri: University of Missouri Press, 1997.

Fred Eugene Leonard: *A Guide to the History of Physical Education*. Philadelphia, Pennsylvania, Lea & Febiger, 1927.

Henry Wadsworth Longfellow: "Songo River." *The Poetical Works of Henry Wadsworth Longfellow in Six Volumes*. Boston, Massachusetts: Houghton, Mifflin and Company, Volume III, p. 97.

Marie Ida de Sion: *Sion! Long May Her Banner Wave! Memories of Notre Dame de Sion in Kansas City 1912–1965 and the Fifty Golden Years of Sister Marie Ida de Sion 1915–1965*. Kansas City, Missouri: April 22, 1965.

Benedict F. Massell: *Rheumatic Fever and Streptococcal Infection*. Boston, Massachusetts: Boston Medical Library Press (Countway Library of Medicine), 1997.

Ralph Melnick: *Senda Berenson: The Unlikely Founder of Women's Basketball*. Amherst, Massachusetts: University of Massachusetts Press, 2007.

Michael A. Meyer: *Response to Modernity: A History of the Reform Movement in Judaism*. Detroit, Michigan: Wayne State University Press, 1988.

Susan A. Miller: *Growing Girls: The Natural Origins of Girls' Organizations in America*. New Brunswick, New Jersey: Rutgers University Press, 2007.

Brian Morris: *Ernest Thompson Seton: Founder of the Woodcraft Indian Movement 1860–1946; Apostle of Indian Wisdom and Pioneer Ecologist*. Lewiston, New York: Edwin Mellen Press, 2007.

Keith A. Murray: "The Trail Smelter Case: International Air Pollution in the Columbia Valley." *British Columbia Studies*. Volume 15, 1972, pp. 68–85.

A Nineteenth Century Miracle: the Brothers Ratisbonne and the Congregation of Notre Dame de Sion. Translated from the French by L. M. Leggatt. London, England: Burns Oates & Washbourne, 1922.

Margaret R. O'Leary and Dennis S. O'Leary: *Tragedy at Graignes: The Bud Sophian Story*. Bloomington, Indiana: IUniverse, 2011.

Wade W. Oliver: *The Man Who Lived for Tomorrow: A Biography of William Hallock Park, MD*. New York City, New York: E.P. Dutton & Company, 1941.

Origins of Sion: Théodore Ratisbonne: Memoirs. Translated by Sister Marian Dolan from the French edition of 1966 containing a long introduction of Mother Marie Alice and the text of Father Théodore's Memoirs. Available at http://www.salvationisfromthejews.com/TRM.pdf; accessed April 1, 2011.

Leslie Paris: *Children's Nature: The Rise of the American Summer Camp*. New York City, New York: New York University Press, 2010.

David Philipson: *The Reform movement in Judaism*. New York City, New York: MacMillan, 1931.

Amanda Porterfield: *American Religious History*. Oxford, England: Blackwell Publishers, 2002.

Rand McNally & Company Auto Road Atlas of the United States and Ontario, Quebec, and the Maritime Provinces of Canada (Chicago, Illinois: Rand McNally & Company, 1927).

Ethel Rogers: *Sebago-Wohelo Camp Fire Girls*. Battle Creek, Michigan: Good Health Publishing Company, 1915.

Albert Dexter Rust: *Record of the Rust Family*: Waco, Texas: Published by the Author, 1891.

Dudley Allen Sargent: *An Autobiography*. Philadelphia, Pennsylvania: Lea and Febiger, 1927.

Dudley Allen Sargent: *Physical Education*. Boston, Massachusetts: Ginn & Company, 1906.

David C. Scott and Brendan Murphy: *The Scouting Party: Pioneering and Preservation, Progressivism and Preparedness in the Boy Scouts of America*. Irving, Texas: Red Honor Press, 2010.

Rod Simpson: *Airlife's World Aircraft*. Shrewsbury, England: Airlife Publishing, 2001.

Ernest Thompson Seton: *Woodcraft and Indian Lore*. New York City, New York: Skyhorse Publishing, 2007.

Moses Foster Sweetser: *The White Mountains: A Handbook for Travellers* [sic]. Boston, Massachusetts: James R. Osgood and Company, 1881.

Elsie Turnbull: *Trail: A Smelter City*. Langley, British Columbia: Sunfire Publications, 1985.

Abigail A. Van Slyck: *A Manufactured Wilderness: Summer Camps and the Shaping of American Youth, 1890–1960*. Minneapolis, Minnesota: University of Minnesota Press, 2010.

Alan Williams: *Republic of Images: A History of French Filmmaking*. Cambridge, Massachusetts: Harvard University Press, 1992.

Alan Williams: *Republic of Images: A History of French Filmmaking*. Cambridge, Massachusetts: Harvard University Press, 1992.

Brenda Wineapple: *Hawthorne: A Life*. New York City, New York: Random House, 2003.

Mark Wischnitzer: *To Dwell in Safety: The Story of Jewish Migration Since 1800*. Philadelphia, Pennsylvania: The Jewish Publication Society of America, 1949.

Index